"SOMETHING INEXPLICABLE IS HAPPENING IN THIS SECTOR, AND IT IS REACHING EPIDEMIC PROPORTIONS."

Kirk nodded. "Klingon ships are disappearing."

"Not just Klingons," Favere replied. "Romulans, and even Federation ships."

Kirk glanced at the report the commodore had handed him, then passed it along to Spock. The report said that ships were literally vanishing without a trace. They didn't have time to radio a distress call back to base or to drop a marker buoy. No wreckage, not even molecular or energy traces remained.

Spock looked up from the report and said, "Excuse me, Commodore, but no doubt you have noticed the single critical piece of information this report *does* contain."

"What is it, Spock?" Kirk asked.

"We know very little about the Klingon or Romulan fleet̲s̲,̲ ̲o̲f̲ ̲c̲o̲urse, but if the Starfleet disappearances cont̲i̲n̲u̲e̲ ̲a̲t̲ ̲t̲h̲e̲ ̲p̲r̲e̲s̲e̲nt rate, the Federation will be w̲i̲t̲h̲o̲u̲t̲ ̲s̲h̲i̲p̲s̲ ̲i̲n̲ ̲t̲w̲o̲ solar years."

Look for STAR TREK Fiction from Pocket Books

Star Trek: The Original Series

Star Trek: The Next Generation

Star Trek: Deep Space Nine

STAR TREK®

THE STARSHIP TRAP

MEL GILDEN

POCKET BOOKS

New York London Toronto Sydney Tokyo Singapore

An *Original* Publication of POCKET BOOKS

POCKET BOOKS, a division of Simon & Schuster Inc.
1230 Avenue of the Americas, New York, NY 10020

This book is published by Pocket Books, a division of Simon & Schuster Inc., under exclusive license from Paramount Pictures.

ISBN: 0-671-79324-1

First Pocket Books printing April 1993

10 9 8 7 6 5 4 3 2 1

Printed in the U.S.A.

For Cathy Clark,
true fan, and constant clipper

To see a world in a grain of sand,
And a heaven in a wild flower,
Hold infinity in the palm of your hand,
And eternity in an hour.

William Blake
1757–1827

Chapter One

CAPTAIN JAMES T. KIRK SAID, "The thing I like most about this job is that I'm never bored." He took a sip of the food replicator memory bank version of coffee and watched the two men who sat near him—Mr. Spock (his Vulcan first name was unpronounceable by humans) and Dr. Leonard McCoy.

The Starship *Enterprise,* presently moored to Starbase 23 by a light tractor beam, was manned by a relaxed and somewhat tired skeleton crew. Most of them were enjoying Starbase 23's limited but welcome opportunities for entertainment.

Captain Kirk was among the few crew members left aboard. He felt entitled to make the command decision that for the moment, even taking shore leave was too much trouble. Kirk assumed that his first officer and his chief medical officer felt the same way, or they would not have been there.

They were taking their ease at a table in the part of the Deck 6 rec room that was designated as officers' country. Except for the fact that the tables were somewhat closer to the intercom and to the food slots than the tables of the enlisted personnel, officers' country was not very different from the rest of the compartment.

While Spock and McCoy considered Kirk's statement he pondered further on why he and his friends had gathered there instead of joining the shore parties on Starbase 23. None of them were prone to avoid an activity merely because doing it involved taking action. Some other factor was at work in this case.

One factor was the pleasure Kirk felt in marking time among the sounds, smells, and energies where a great deal of concentration and responsibility was normally demanded of him. However, he finally decided the real reason they were all still there was that none of them gave up responsibility easily, and they felt obligated to stay close to their stations even when their stations did not need them.

Spock was considering Kirk's statement—seriously, as usual. Though—or perhaps because—his intelligence was well off the scale in human terms, he had little capacity for small talk.

McCoy, on the other hand, was always ready for a friendly scrap. "Personally," he said gruffly—McCoy often spoke gruffly—"after what we've been through, I look forward to a little boredom." Like Kirk, McCoy was drinking coffee. Spock preferred an obscure blend of Vulcan tea, also with a name unpronounceable by humans.

Spock said, "Just as I do not understand the human tendency to use up great quantities of energy when supposedly resting on vacation, I do not understand the occasional human desire for a lack of mental stimulation."

"You understand it all right, Spock," McCoy said. "But when *you* do it, you call it meditating."

Spock was long past being offended by anything McCoy said, but he sometimes allowed himself to be baited for the entertainment value of the discussion. Kirk listened with only half an ear while Spock explained meditation and its applications to Vulcan philosophy.

The bosun's whistle sounded, and a female voice came over the intercom. "Bridge to Captain Kirk."

Spock stopped speaking. As he crossed the compartment to the intercom Kirk felt his dissatisfaction growing. He was miffed at having been interrupted at doing not much of anything at all. He hit the button and said, "Yes, Ensign—Miraskin, is it?"

"Yes, sir. Is that you, Captain?"

Kirk wondered where these off-watch kids came from. Gently he said, "Yes, Ensign, it's me. What's the problem?"

"An emergency message has just arrived from Starfleet."

Kirk covered the intercom grid with one hand and said to Spock and McCoy, "Probably an admiral with a hangnail." Into the intercom he said, "Read it to me."

"I can't, sir. It's Eyes Only."

"Damn."

"What was that, sir?"

"Nothing, Ensign. Send it to my cabin. Kirk out." He punched the button again and turned to shrug at Spock and McCoy. "What can I do? Starfleet can't get along without me."

"Let me know if you need any help with that hangnail," McCoy called after him as the door shushed closed.

The corridor was silent but for the hiss of the air circulators and his own footsteps. Even the constant thrum of the engines was absent. Scotty had shut them down so they could be checked and tuned. He had wanted to do the checking and tuning himself, but McCoy had forced him to take shore leave by threatening to impose a one-month medical leave during which time Scotty would not be allowed to touch an engine.

As he walked Kirk felt the immense size and mass of his ship pressing in on him, squeezing the mechanical artery through which he moved. He did not feel this way often; normally the ship was more an extension of himself than a big machine. But empty, drawing its power from a starbase, its self-sufficiency momentarily gone, everything spiritual about the *Enterprise* was different. Kirk smiled. Did the ship have a spirit? He would like to see Spock and McCoy argue that one.

Kirk got to his cabin without meeting anybody. Inside he hurriedly sat at his desk and punched his private security code into the intercom console. The Starfleet insignia came up on the screen and then a request that he further identify himself. While he waited for the machine to read his retinal pattern he wondered what this was all about. If he needed to go through all this rigmarole, it must be something important. Curiosity gnawed at him until the machine said "Thank you" and the message came up at last.

A Starfleet officer Kirk didn't know looked out at him. He was very thin and had an immense bush of black hair that covered not only the top of his head but his forehead as well. Perhaps he wasn't entirely human. No matter. In a nervous voice the man said, "I am Lieutenant Lungo. Admiral Nogura has asked me to give you the following orders. Please proceed soonest to Pegasus IV, where you are to follow without question the instructions of Conrad Franklin Kent or his representative."

"We've been on patrol for months, Lieutenant. My people deserve a little R and R. What's this all about?"

Lungo looked at something offscreen and then smiled at Kirk without sincerity. What the hell was going on here? Kirk wondered. Why had Nogura sent this nervous lieutenant instead of speaking with Kirk himself? Lungo said, "I'm sorry, Captain. That is all the information I have." The screen went blank. End of discussion.

Kirk drummed his fingers in frustration on the desk. His people were tired. Dammit, *he* was tired. The crew of the *Enterprise* deserved a rest. Still, when duty called Kirk could do nothing but answer it. Nogura had not become a Starfleet admiral by acting capriciously.

The thing that upset Kirk the most was the identity

of his prospective passenger. He had heard of Conrad Franklin Kent—who in the Federation hadn't? Kent was a senior member of the Federation Council with unconcealed ambitions for the presidency. And Kent was no friend of Starfleet. At the least provocation he would assure anyone in earshot that Starfleet was an outmoded, warmongering, self-serving institution full of half-bright egomaniacs. Kirk had no use for him, but Kent obviously had friends in high places. The urgency of the order meant that Kent had probably gotten himself into trouble that Kirk would be required to get him out of. And Kent would certainly not be grateful. Kirk shook his head. Orders were orders, but he didn't have to like them.

Kirk hit the intercom button, and the face of Ensign Miraskin filled the screen. She was a young, dark-haired woman with strong cheekbones and a jaw like a lantern. Uhura was probably doing her a favor by giving her bridge experience. Kirk ordered her to recall all personnel; they were to prepare for immediate departure. He made particular reference to Mr. Scott, who should be delighted, Kirk felt, that it was necessary for him to start the engines.

Aboard shuttles and by transporter beams they came. Grumbling and cursing they came. Quickly the mixture of men, women, and aliens filled the ship like a multicolored fluid: red shirts for engineering and support services, blue shirts for the sciences, and gold shirts for command. The members of the crew took their stations, still grumbling, but with absolute competence and reliability.

As the ship filled, Kirk's mood improved because the *Enterprise* felt more and more like herself. Crew members hurried through the increasingly crowded corridors, each engrossed in his or her small part of the business of running a starship. Mr. Scott's engines maintained a constant bass note.

In less than one day ship's time, when everyone was at a station and the *Enterprise* was ready for travel, Kirk stood next to his command chair and spoke to his crew over the intercom. He said, "This is the captain speaking. I understand that some of you are not very happy about having your shore leave cut short. The truth is, I'm not very happy about it myself." When he noticed Spock watching him, Spock quickly peered into his library viewer. Kirk went on, "But we have a job to do, and I expect that each of you will be equal to the task. Kirk out."

Shortly they were on their way to Pegasus IV at warp six, and no one had much to do till they arrived. Kirk had no idea what Kent's problem was, so there was no way for him to prepare for that. But Spock was helpful filling in details about Pegasus IV.

Spock pulled the receiver from his ear and said, "Pegasus IV is a warm place by human standards, with a mean daytime temperature in the temperate zones of thirty-seven degrees Celsius. The atmosphere is barely breathable, being full of ash, and of chemicals that on Earth are found only in laboratories. The surface is mostly rock. I understand that natural weathering by the corrosive wind and volcanic activity has carved some of it into sculptures that are quite beautiful."

Kirk smiled and said, "I doubt if Mr. Kent is there for the scenery, Mr. Spock."

"Indeed not, Captain. The natives of Pegasus IV are also quite interesting. They are known as G'lops, and they are well adapted to their geologically active planet. Each of them seems to be no more than a quantity of brightly colored mud bubbling in its own small crater. Early survey teams established that the G'lops were intelligent, though measured on an entirely different scale from humanoids."

"So Kent is there looking for political talent."

"Possible, Captain, but unlikely. Pegasus IV is not yet a member of the Federation. Its natives cannot sit on the council because they are not citizens."

Spock claimed that Vulcans neither bluffed nor lied. Yet Kirk always found it amazing that Spock could say things like that with a straight face. He suspected a Vulcan sense of humor, or at least a sense of the ridiculous. Spock denied understanding either one except as an intellectual concept. Kirk said, "My mistake, Mr. Spock. Why is he there?"

"I believe he is interested in the mineral rights. According to surveys, the planet is well over ten percent daystromite."

So that's what prevented Pegasus IV from remaining a footnote in galactic history. Daystromite was a crystal used in the transtator, the fundamental component in almost every piece of Federation technology. A thought chilled Kirk. He said, "A find like that should bring the Klingons out of the woodwork. Could that be Mr. Kent's problem?"

"Possibly. Klingon warships have been detected at the edge of this sector."

Kirk turned away from Spock and said, "Uhura, see

if you can raise anybody on Pegasus IV. If there are Klingons around, I don't want to be the last to know."

"Aye, Captain." Kirk barely had time to return to his command chair and sit down before Uhura said, "I've contacted a Dr. Brewster, the supervisor of the team on Pegasus IV."

"On screen."

The starfield on the main viewscreen rippled and was replaced by what appeared to be a small boulder. It stood against an angry red sky that roiled over stages and pedestals of cracked and blasted rock all the way to the far horizon. In a surprisingly sweet voice the boulder said, "I am Dr. Brewster."

It was a horta, of course. Who else but a rock creature would the Federation send out to speak with pools of intelligent mud? "This is James T. Kirk, captain of the Starship *Enterprise*. What is your status?"

"Status, Captain?"

"Does a state of emergency exist? Are you in any danger? From Klingons, for example."

"We are in no danger. We are progressing nicely with the G'lops."

Curiouser and curiouser. "What about Mr. Kent?"

"Mr. Kent and party are fine, too. He has been most emphatic about leaving. Are you, perhaps, here to assist him?"

The horta actually sounded eager. Evidently Mr. Kent was spreading sunshine wherever he went. Kirk said, "Can I speak with Mr. Kent?"

"Of course." With a sound of stone against gravel Dr. Brewster slid out of range of the subspace radio.

In a moment a human took his place. The human wore a breather, a semipermeable membrane that was nearly invisible over his face. He was a big man who had obviously been a guest at too many formal dinners and did most of his work sitting down. His white hair was piled like tiny feathers on his head and fell over his ears. He wore a diplomat's gray jumpsuit with the Federation insignia on one shoulder.

Kent nodded at Kirk and said, "I am Conrad Franklin Kent, sir. You must be our ride to Starbase 12."

Ride to Starbase 12? Had the *Enterprise* actually been dragged away from a well-deserved rest in order to haul this politician to his next whistle stop? No wonder Nogura wouldn't speak to Kirk personally. The old campaigner was probably embarrassed as hell.

Kirk said, "In a manner of speaking, sir, I suppose that's true. I am Captain James Kirk of the Federation Starship *Enterprise*. We were on leave when——"

Kent smiled and said, "I know who you are. Payton, my aide, specifically requested the *Enterprise* to transport us."

Kent was a very smooth customer, which immediately put Kirk off. For one thing, though Kirk could be smooth himself when it seemed called for, he preferred sincerity to snake oil. For another thing, Kirk had never fancied himself a taxi driver. He said, "Surely the *Enterprise* was not the only ship available to you."

"I'm sorry, Captain, but Payton generally gets what she wants."

This was maddening, to have been dragged screaming and kicking away from Starbase 23 at the whim of some spoiled civilian! And not even by the man himself, but by his assistant! Kirk attempted to contain his anger. Considering Kent's attitude toward Starfleet, the fact that he'd disturbed one of its officers might be a great source of pleasure to him. Kirk said, "Mr. Sulu, what is our ETA at Pegasus IV?"

"Eight hours, fourteen minutes, sir."

Brusquely Kirk said to Kent, "We will arrive in eight hours. Please see that you and your party are ready to leave at that time. Kirk out." He flicked a hand signal at Uhura, and she ended the transmission.

Spock said, "Anger is illogical, Captain."

"Perhaps, Spock. But sometimes it's all you have."

Eight hours and fourteen minutes later the *Enterprise* made standard orbit around Pegasus IV. From space it was an angry ball that matched Kirk's mood exactly. Spock reported no Klingons within sensor range. All seemed well, except for the fact that the *Enterprise* was there at all.

Kirk and Spock went to the transporter room to welcome Kent and party. "Though," Kirk said, "that does seem to be beyond the scope of our orders."

Mr. Scott glanced in their direction and tried to hide a smile. Word about why leave had been cut short had gotten around the ship. Mr. Kent and party were not popular aboard the *Enterprise*.

"I would advise you to restrain your disapproval, Captain," said Spock. "A man such as Kent is already inclined to think the worst of Starfleet. Rudeness will not improve the situation."

Spock was undoubtedly correct, and yet Kirk could

not help wondering if Spock hadn't been contemplating a little rudeness himself. After all, *his* leave had been interrupted, too. With a straight face Kirk said, "I would never go so far as to be rude, Mr. Spock." One of Spock's eyebrows rose, indicating that while he did not exactly believe Kirk, he was willing to accept the captain's statement for harmony's sake.

"Mr. Kent and party signal ready."

Kirk had a here-we-go feeling when he said, "Beam them aboard, Mr. Scott."

The air above the transporter stage fizzed, and a moment later two people descended to the floor of the transporter room. One, with his hand outstretched in greeting, was Conrad Franklin Kent. The other was a stunning dark-haired woman who stood to one side. She was dressed in much the same way as Kent, with the addition of a shapeless lump of a hat on her head.

Kirk perked up right away. Though he did not like Kent, he approved of Kent's taste in associates. Could this be the famous Payton, the one who'd actually arranged to have the *Enterprise* travel to Pegasus IV?

Kirk introduced himself and Mr. Spock as they shook hands all around. The woman was in fact Kent's senior aide, Hazel Payton.

Kirk smiled at Payton and said, "You must be 'and party.'"

"What?"

"As in Conrad Franklin Kent 'and party.'"

She studied Kirk for a moment with cool disbelief. Kirk wondered if perhaps he'd laid on the charm a little thick. The question was, why was he laying on the charm at all? This woman worked for a political enemy of Starfleet, and she had been responsible for giving Kirk one of the sorriest assignments of his career. He clapped his hands together once and said, "Allow me to show you to your cabins. Mr. Scott, call the bridge and have Mr. Sulu make best speed for Starbase 12."

"Aye, Captain."

They walked to the turbolift in pairs, Kirk and Kent leading Spock and Payton. Spock said to Kent, "I am most interested to know your impressions of the work being done on Pegasus IV."

Seriously, almost conspiratorially, Kent explained. "As Brewster said, it's progressing nicely. But I never would have known it if I'd stayed on Earth. I grew impatient with the vagueness of the reports I was getting, so I went to take a look-see for myself. Payton set the whole thing up."

"She seems to do that a lot," Kirk said. He glanced back at her. She seemed to remain unaffected by the fact that they were talking about her.

Kent looked at Kirk quizzically and made a single breathy laugh. "Has she rubbed you the wrong way, Captain?"

"Perhaps not rubbed," Kirk said cautiously.

"I warn you, Captain. Hazel Payton is a woman who *gets the job done*. Her ethics are occasionally called into question, but never her results. Isn't that right, Ms. Payton?"

"I do my best, sir."

Kirk said, "As long as everyone remembers whose ship this is."

"We are civilians, Captain. Starfleet bluster will not avail you."

Before Kirk could think of a brilliant rejoinder he

would try to be sorry for later, Spock said, "Our destination is Starbase 12. I know of nothing there that merits a 'look-see.'"

They waited at the end of the corridor for a few seconds, and then the turbolift came. They stepped inside, Kirk said, "Deck 5," and it rose. No one spoke. Kirk didn't like Payton or her boss. He didn't like being a messenger boy. And he didn't care why they were going to Starbase 12. He wanted only to get there safely, beam over his passengers, and go about his business.

On Deck 5 Kirk decided that as angry as he was, he could not entirely ignore his responsibilities as host. "There are observation windows in the lounge, as well as food replicator slots. There are also food slots in each of your cabins."

"We are familiar with starship geography," Payton said.

Kirk took a deep breath and let it out slowly. He said, "Here are your cabins. If they're not satisfactory, let Mr. Spock or me know, and we'll try to remedy the problem."

"I'm sure they're the best you have," Kent said. He looked warily in through the open doorway, as if expecting to share the cabin with a wild animal.

Kirk smiled without heat and escaped as quickly as he could with Mr. Spock at his side. In the turbolift Spock said, "Mr. Kent did not respond regarding Starbase 12."

"As far as he is concerned, that is probably not Starfleet business. And perhaps he's right."

"Perhaps." Spock clasped his hands behind his back and gazed at the turbolift doors. Kirk knew

Spock was thinking hard about something. He trusted Spock to tell him what it was when the time was right.

Not an hour later Kirk was on the bridge wondering if he and his passengers would survive the next three days. Personally, he intended to have as little as possible to do with them. Not even Payton, as beautiful as she was, was worth the trouble of getting to know better. He decided he could handle three days, but he was glad that the trip to Starbase 12 was not longer.

A yeoman brought Kirk a memoboard with a message on it from Hazel Payton. According to the message, he and his senior staff were invited to a reception for Conrad Franklin Kent, to be held that evening in the Deck 5 officers' lounge. The woman was insufferable!

Kirk's first impulse was to forbid the reception, but on further reflection he could think of no good reason it should not happen. Kent had warned him that Payton's methods were unorthodox. If this was the worst she could do—throwing an unauthorized party —Kirk had little to worry about. Maybe if he was charming enough, it would have a positive effect on Kent. The attempt could not hurt.

Mr. Spock said, "Anything wrong, Captain?"

"Not at all, Mr. Spock. We've been invited to a reception for Conrad Franklin Kent."

"Indeed?"

"Meaning?"

"Nothing at all, Captain. I was merely acknowledging that I'd heard you."

Kirk nodded. Perhaps not knowing why Kent and

party were going to Starbase 12 bothered him more than he liked to admit. He'd hoped that Spock had somehow deduced an answer. Evidently Spock had not. Not yet.

"Captain," Sulu said, "I'm picking up a craft at extreme sensor range."

"Identify," said Kirk.

Spock began touching controls on his board. He looked into the blue light of his readout and said, "Identification difficult at this range, Captain, but it appears to be a single Klingon vessel."

"Go to yellow alert," Kirk ordered, and the Klaxon sounded. McCoy was wrong. The excitement he felt in his veins was preferable to boredom anytime.

Chapter Two

As DANGEROUS AS THEY WERE, Kirk preferred Klingons to Federation council members who had an inflated view of their own importance. You always knew where you stood with a Klingon. Whereas a politician was, at best, unpredictable.

Sulu said, "Klingon vessel now at sublight. Five hundred thousand kilometers and closing."

"Tactical," Kirk called.

The stars on the main viewscreen wavered and were replaced by a computer-generated chart showing the relative positions of the *Enterprise,* the Klingon ship, and the nearest major natural bodies.

If there had been more than one Klingon ship, Kirk would have assumed that the *Enterprise* was under attack and would soon be embroiled in battle. But a

17

single Klingon ship could mean anything, and Kirk did not want to be the one to fire the first shot if firing was not necessary.

"Sensors, Mr. Spock."

"From the little we know about Klingon engineering, power curves indicate the ship is apparently in normal running mode. Only navigational shields are in use, no power to weapons."

"That's good news." Kirk rubbed his chin and wondered what was going on. These Klingons wanted something, and if it wasn't a fight, what was it? He could ask Spock for an opinion, but undoubtedly Spock would tell him that data was insufficient to allow speculation.

Someone came onto the bridge, but, engrossed as he was in the tactical display, Kirk did not pay attention.

"What is the meaning of this, Kirk? Why are we under yellow alert?"

At the sound of Kent's voice Kirk became angry. He said, "I don't have time to explain now."

"I insist. Are we under attack?"

Kirk shot Kent a hard stare and saw that Payton stood next to him. He said, "Get off my bridge," but he didn't take time to enjoy the surprised expression on Kent's face. Kirk turned his attention back to the viewscreen.

Uhura said, "We're being hailed by the Klingon ship, sir."

Kirk swallowed hard and said, "On screen, Lieutenant."

The tactical display was replaced by a Klingon who had a long, thin nose and a spot of beard that barely covered his chin. Kirk had seen Klingons smile—

generally at someone else's expense—but this one was not doing it. Angrily he said, "I am Torm, commander of the Klingon warship *Kormak*."

Kirk stood up and introduced himself. His body was tensed and ready for a fight, as if he were meeting Torm in the flesh instead of seeing him through a device that allowed them to talk tough at each other while many thousands of kilometers apart. Behind him Kent said, "Captain."

Damn, Kirk thought, the man was still there. Could Kent be what the Klingons wanted? If he was, and if they knew where to get him, their intelligence reports were terrifyingly accurate and up-to-date. But it was too early to worry about any of that. All this flashed through Kirk's mind while he blinked once.

Kirk said, "This is Federation space, Torm. What do you want?"

"Your pretense of innocence is not convincing, Kirk. We want our ships back."

"Back? Back from where?"

"From wherever your Earthers have taken them!" Torm shouted nastily.

"I don't know what you're talking about."

"Our ships are disappearing without a trace, Kirk. Who but the Federation has both the technology and the desire to do such a thing?"

Kirk glanced at Spock, who shook his head. The Klingon commander obviously had a problem— which was no skin off Kirk's nose—and it was a relief to discover that it had nothing to do with Conrad Franklin Kent. Perhaps the Klingon's spy network was no better than the Federation's after all. "It's a big galaxy, Torm. The Klingons must have many enemies.

If the Federation had declared war on the Klingon Empire, I would know about it."

"Captain," Kent said, and he stepped down to where Kirk stood. While Torm studied them through narrow eyes Kent whispered belligerently, "You hot-shots in Starfleet think you're the only ones capable of dealing with Klingons. I believe that a little common sense and understanding will go a lot further than phasers and photon torpedoes."

He had to admire Kent's courage, but that did not prevent Kirk from considering him a first-rate ass. In Kirk's experience, Klingons understood nothing *but* phasers and photon torpedoes. He answered, also in a whisper, "Please allow the professionals to handle this." He turned back to Torm, opened his mouth to deny the allegation once again, and found Kent speaking already.

Kent said, "We admit nothing about the weapon."

"I knew it," Torm said.

As if it were actually receding into the distance, Kirk saw the situation getting away from him. He wondered wildly if he should follow Kent's lead. The man's words would have the Klingons spending time and energy looking for a new Federation weapon that didn't even exist. That had a certain appeal, but Kirk wasn't convinced that the situation had yet become dire enough to justify lying. Besides—and it was a big besides—if the Klingons believed the Federation had attacked their ships, with a new weapon or no, they had a right to believe a state of war existed, and to act accordingly. Kent was putting the *Enterprise* in danger with his bluster.

Kent was obviously not going to cooperate with

Kirk, yet it was necessary to show a unified front. Kirk was forced to be the adult. He said, "As I said before, you're in Federation space. You'd better leave before somebody drops a house on you, too."

"House?" asked Torm. "Drops a house?"

"An old Earther expression," Kirk said offhandedly. Behind him he heard Uhura chuckling. "End transmission, Lieutenant."

The screen returned to the tactical display.

"View forward," Kirk said.

On the viewscreen the looming cobra form of the *Kormak* obstructed the stars for a moment and then shot away, impulse engines glowing. Kirk canceled the yellow alert.

"Well, Captain," said Kent, "I'm pleased that you saw fit to come around at last."

Kirk turned to Kent and glared directly into his eyes. With menace he said, "I don't care who you are, Mr. Kent, or how well you're connected. If ever again you enter my bridge without being invited, I will clap you in irons. Is that clear?"

Payton was still standing at the turbolift door. She said, "It's clear that you haven't the capacity to be grateful."

Kirk saw the smile playing around Kent's lips when he said, "Very well, Captain. I will tolerate your order for now." He and Payton turned to leave.

Kirk said, "A moment, Mr. Kent."

"What now, Captain? Is there another part of the ship you'd care to bar me from?"

"I hope the bridge will be sufficient. Tell me about the weapon about which you admit nothing."

Kent laughed so hard he could not speak. When he

was done, he said, "There is no weapon. It is entirely a figment of my imagination."

Spock said, "Captain Torm claims that Klingon ships are disappearing."

"The fact that the Klingons cannot keep track of their ships is neither my problem nor Starfleet's."

Kirk said, "It is Starfleet's problem if the Klingons believe Starfleet is responsible."

Kent seemed stunned by Kirk's remark. But he recovered and said, "I assure you, Captain, that the situation you fear can be avoided using normal diplomatic channels."

"I have no great faith in diplomacy where Klingons are involved, but I hope for all of our sakes that you are right."

"Yes, yes, Captain," Kent said impatiently. "Is there anything else before I leave your bridge forever?"

Kirk had a few suggestions, but none of them were either suitable for the bridge or practical. He said, "Thank you for your help, Mr. Kent." Kirk looked at Mr. Sulu and said, "Resume course to Starbase 12."

"Aye, Captain."

As Kirk sat down in his command chair Kent and Payton left the bridge. Soon Spock came down to stand at his side. He said, "Captain, I know of no Earth proverb concerning the dropping of houses."

Kirk smiled and said, "Tell him, Uhura."

"It's not a proverb, Mr. Spock. The captain was referring to a classic children's novel called *The Wizard of Oz*. In it the heroine arrives in a fantasy world aboard her farmhouse, which falls out of the sky onto a wicked witch."

"Fascinating," Spock said with amazement.

"I believe it is based on a Russian fairy tale," Chekov said thoughtfully. "It concerns a tractor falling out of the sky onto an evil commissar."

"The text is available in the ship's memory banks," Uhura said.

"Thank you, Lieutenant. I will view it at my earliest opportunity."

Spock was about to return to his station when Kirk asked him, "Are Klingon ships really disappearing?"

"Information on the Klingon fleet is extremely fragmentary. But it is difficult to see how the Klingons would benefit by claiming such a thing if it were not so."

"In that case, their question is a good one. If the Federation is not responsible, then who?"

"Unknown, Captain. But the possibilities are intriguing."

"A little too intriguing for my taste, Spock. Whatever it is, it's obviously a force to be reckoned with. I hope that when our time comes we make out better than the Klingons."

Spock said nothing. At the moment there was nothing to say.

Kirk shook his head. "I can't help feeling that Conrad Franklin Kent knows more than he is telling about all this."

"He certainly attempted to convey that impression to the Klingons."

Kirk disliked the possibility that Kent was being more truthful to the Klingons than to him. He said, "Uhura, contact Starfleet Command. Give them a full report on our contact with the *Kormak* and request current information on the disappearance of Klingon vessels. Send it tight beam and scramble."

"Aye, Captain."

"The answer should be most enlightening," Spock said.

"I hope so, Spock. I hope so."

Kent was in his cabin preparing for the reception when a chime announced the presence of someone at his door. His visitor was Hazel Payton, now dressed in a personal energy field that sparkled, revealing more or less of her as she moved. The field flowed from a button clinging to her left shoulder. In her hair was a peculiar jeweled accessory.

"I see," Kent said, "that you are dressed to meet and beguile the enemy."

"As far as I know," Payton said, "there will be no Klingons at this reception."

"No Klingons, no." With one finger he pushed around some decorative pins held in a small box.

"Kirk isn't our enemy, Conrad."

"He is Starfleet. Just like that young man of yours on Starbase 12. Starfleet is an even more insidious enemy of the Federation than the Klingons because they have fooled so many into supporting them." He lifted a simple pearl pin from the box and pressed it into the center of the white triangle of pleats that showed above his gray coat.

"Which is why you feel it commendable to cooperate with Professor Omen."

"Not just commendable, but necessary."

"Meanwhile—"

"Meanwhile," Kent said, "we have a reception to attend."

"That's actually the reason I'm here, Conrad. I came to see if you were ready for our grand entrance."

Kent nodded and said, "We've been all through this before, anyway." He picked up a tall glass from a side table. In it was a blue liquid with red bubbles that trailed to the surface and broke, releasing a scent of cinnamon. "Very clever of you," Kent said, "to arrange our meeting with Professor Omen on Starbase 12." He sipped, then smacked his lips once.

Payton shrugged. "You said yourself I'm a woman who gets things done."

"I say it because it's true. Which is why I keep you around despite your regrettable politics."

"My falling in love with a Starfleet officer is not a political statement."

"So you've said." He took another sip of the blue liquid, put down the glass, and asked for his cape.

Payton shook her head as she smiled ruefully and lifted the short black cape from the back of a chair. She draped it across Kent's shoulders, and when she reached around to close it in the front Kent took her hands tenderly in his and said, "You know I want only the best for you."

"I know. But we both sometimes forget that I am only your aide, not your daughter." She kissed him on the cheek and then pulled away. "Come on. We'll be late."

Kirk arrived at the reception a little late, hoping that Kent and Payton would already be there, but he was disappointed. He wondered if it was an accident or a calculated ploy that *they* would be the ones who would arrive fashionably *late enough*. He smiled at himself; he was thinking like a politician, not like a Starfleet officer. What real difference could it possibly make who arrived when?

Probably at Payton's request, the Starfleet insignia on the wall had been covered with an artfully draped cloth. A long table had been set up at one end of the lounge and covered with bits of food on trays. Bottles containing beverages with active ingredients such as alcohol, kebo, and sabora stood together before a yeoman from the kitchen staff, looking like an alien city. The bottles were red, brown, yellow, and blue. One could get anything from brown bottles of Bass, a beer made on Earth, to something called Altairian devil, after the gently glowing and tentacled life-form that floated alive inside the twisted green bottle. Kirk had tried it once and had paid for his experiment by listening to screams only he could hear for the next day and a half. Some people liked it. He couldn't imagine why.

Almost everyone was already there. Spock was talking with McCoy. They liked to pretend they hated each other, but, like a bickering married couple, each would feel incomplete if alone for long. Their differences of opinion frequently made Kirk's job easier by allowing him to examine all sides of an issue before making a decision.

Lieutenant Uhura, head of communications, was apparently telling a rowdy story to Lieutenant Commander Montgomery Scott, *Enterprise*'s chief engineer, and to Chekov and Sulu. Chekov was Kirk's first navigator, and Sulu was the best helmsman in the fleet. Strictly speaking, neither of them was the head of a department, but they were frequently dragooned into service at social functions to fill out the crowd. Now that Kirk had arrived, only Kent and Payton were missing.

Kirk got himself a glass of Chablis and joined Spock and McCoy. "Gentlemen," he said, and he nodded to them.

McCoy saluted him with a glass that probably contained something substantial and southern. "Swell party," he said, "but from the looks of the guest list, we could have held it on the bridge."

"The party wasn't my idea. If you don't like the way it's being run, I suggest you complain to Ms. Payton."

McCoy grinned and said with admiration, "What a woman."

"Appearances aren't everything."

"A strange sentiment coming from the man who still holds the Starfleet Academy record in certain unofficial competitions."

Spock looked at Kirk inquisitively.

"I was really good at checkers," Kirk said. He sipped his wine and pointed a finger at McCoy. "That woman's methods are unorthodox, to say the least. Look at us, torn away from our well-deserved leave to ferry Payton and her boss to Starbase 12. And look at this party. It's my ship, but this is her party."

"Unorthodox, huh?" asked McCoy. "Kind of reminds me of a captain named Kirk."

"No need to be insulting, Bones."

"Yesterday you might have said I was paying you a compliment."

"That was yesterday." Kirk knew that he did not always play by Starfleet rules, but it seemed to him that he always had a good reason for doing what he did. As far as he was concerned, Payton's reasons were open to question. The fact that she worked for Kent was particularly suspicious in that respect.

Kirk was about to tell McCoy so when he became aware that the conversation around them had stopped. He looked toward the door and saw Kent and Payton making their entrance. He shook his head; they were vanity and game-playing personified.

Kirk nodded at them but refused to greet them at the door. It was Payton's party; let her greet him. As they strolled around the room speaking with the other guests Kirk logged and noted that McCoy had been right about one thing, anyway. Payton really was a very beautiful woman.

Casually Kirk said, "Unusual piece of jewelry in Ms. Payton's hair."

Spock said, "I believe, Captain, that you are referring to her memory augmentation/cranial interface."

Kirk tried not to stare. "I've heard of them, of course, but I've never actually seen one."

The interface allowed a memory chip to be plugged directly into the brain. The chip would instantly give one access to a foreign language, higher mathematics, the rules of three-dimensional chess—a whole library of chips was available. Kirk was relieved when he had learned that one did not necessarily *understand* the information on the chip. For instance, one could be supplied with a chip containing everything Starfleet knew about being the captain of a Constitution-class starship. But without training the raw information would be useless, just as without the proper preparation one could read a textbook on trigonometry without understanding it.

"It's a relatively simple surgical procedure, really," McCoy said. "Come on down to sickbay some afternoon, Spock, and I'll do it for you."

"Vulcans do not mutilate themselves in that way. We prefer to train the mind rather than artificially enhance it."

"Amazing that you consent to fly through space in something as artificial as a starship."

"I submit, Doctor, that the situations are hardly parallel."

McCoy shrugged but continued to smile. Evidently he felt that he'd won a round. Spock's expression was unreadable.

While Spock and McCoy had been arguing, Kirk had been watching Kent and Payton. They had chosen to drink Saurian brandy, and now they were joking with Uhura and the others. Evidently Kent could be quite gracious when it suited him. He didn't care what opinion Kirk had of him, but Kent obviously thought it wise to stay friendly with the staff.

Soon Kent and Payton made an excuse of some sort and approached Kirk. When they came within hailing distance Kirk said, "What a lovely party."

"Yes," said Kent. "Your starship facilities are surprisingly civilized."

Kirk felt his smile hardening on his face. He said, "How very kind. We're planning to put in electricity and running water any day now."

Kent seemed to have been stunned by Kirk's words. Then he laughed heartily and said, "You do not agree with my views on Starfleet, Captain, but you must admit that some of my arguments have merit."

"I admit that you have arguments that seem good to you. Nothing more."

"Look at the evidence, Kirk. Starfleet is always fighting with somebody—the Klingons, the Romulans, some other, less worthy adversary. Wars of conquest for its own glory are all it knows."

"I believe," Spock said, "the preponderance of the evidence would indicate that you are wrong. Starfleet's reputation as a peacekeeper is well known."

"Well known to its friends on the council, perhaps, but I insist—"

"You can insist all you want to, Councilor," McCoy said, "but I think you have another reason for criticizing Starfleet."

"What might that be?" Payton asked. Her smile was icy.

McCoy said, "You're using Starfleet to give yourself a higher public profile. It's a documented fact that you're bucking to be president of the Federation Council."

Good old Bones, Kirk thought: rushing in where diplomats fear to tread. Still, it was probably just as well that it was McCoy making the suggestion instead of Kirk himself. Being more visible, captains were much more vulnerable to political attack than were doctors. If Kent wanted to get tough, Kirk could lose his ship; McCoy could lose little, no matter that he'd made an enemy of some blowhard councilor.

Kent frowned and Payton looked at him expectantly. Did Kirk notice the smallest smile—a real smile this time—at her lips? She was enjoying Kent's discomfort as much as McCoy was. If she was not the enemy of Starfleet that Kent was, perhaps Kirk could find it in his heart to be interested in her after all.

"Very good, Doctor," Spock whispered. "I am quite surprised at your knowledge of current events."

"You're not the only one around here who reads," McCoy whispered back.

Kent said, "My interest in the presidency does not invalidate my interest in Starfleet, does it, Doctor?" Kirk was amazed how noble Kent could appear.

"Of course not," said McCoy. "But if you want a real cause, an important cause, I'd advise you to stop hurling brickbats at Starfleet and take on the medical establishment."

"Is that so?" Kent asked.

"It is. Were you aware that the methods the Starfleet Medical Corps uses to approve new drugs and medical techniques haven't been updated in over twenty-five years?"

"No, I wasn't." Kent seemed to give the matter real thought.

"You know as well as I do that Starfleet is an instrument of civilization, and that without it the Klingons would be all over us like a cheap suit. I know that medical approval is not the flashy cause the death of Starfleet is, but it is considerably more worthwhile."

"Thank you for your suggestion, Doctor. I will consider it."

After that Kent went to speak with Uhura, and Chekov tried to monopolize Payton. But when he saw that Kirk also had an interest Chekov backed off and got into the discussion of the experimental transwarp drive that Scotty was having with Sulu.

Kirk smiled and said, "Can I get you another drink, Ms. Payton?"

"No, thank you, Captain. I find that a little Saurian brandy goes a long way."

Kirk nodded and watched his people mix. He had the best crew in the fleet, no question about it. Without them the miracles he was sometimes accused of performing would have been impossible for anyone. He looked back at her and said, "I've never seen a cranial interface worn with such style."

"Thank you, Captain."

"Would it be impolite of me to ask what kind of chip you have in at the moment?"

"It would, but since I have nothing to hide, I'll tell you that it is merely a sensory enhancer and pickup. I am making a record of Mr. Kent's activities for his own private use. Everything I see and hear is recorded by equipment back in my cabin. I can make index marks on the recording by thinking of special codes."

"I'm sure that Mr. Spock would be impressed by your mental discipline. Do you expect something of interest to happen at this reception?"

"One never knows. In any case, recording Mr. Kent's activities is standard operating procedure."

"The recording of civilian logs is not standard operating procedure on the *Enterprise,* Ms. Payton."

"I assure you, Captain, that Mr. Kent and I have full Starfleet clearance to operate in this way."

"You do not yet have *my* clearance. Please see that

you limit your recording to public parts of the ship and to activities in your own cabins."

"Of course, sir."

The conversational temperature had fallen many degrees since Kirk had mentioned the interface. In an attempt to raise it again he said, "So how long have you and Mr. Kent been together?"

After thinking for a moment, Payton said, "Four— no, five years."

"You make quite a team."

"We each have a job to do."

"And yours is to *get the job done.*"

A smile broke through Payton's composure, and she and Kirk had a little laugh together.

After a moment Kirk asked, "Do you agree with his views on Starfleet?"

Kirk saw the small opening he'd made vanish. Stiffly Payton said, "My views are of absolutely no importance to anyone but me, Captain. *I* am not a member of the Federation Council."

"I'm sorry. I didn't realize it was a touchy subject."

"Not touchy, Captain, but I resent anyone trying to pry Mr. Kent and me apart. If you will excuse me . . ." She strode across the room and, to Chekov's delight, began to speak with him.

McCoy wandered over and asked, "Any luck, Jim?"

"She's a woman with a lot of spirit," Kirk admitted.

They both drank. And then McCoy said, "What's the word on the Klingons?"

"Word?"

"The scuttlebutt around the ship is that you saved us by performing another miracle. Imagine two of us miracle workers aboard the same ship."

33

"I don't know about your miracles, Bones, but in my case we were lucky. The Klingon captain preferred to go home and report a new Federation secret weapon rather than fight."

"What new secret weapon?"

"The one that's been destroying Klingon ships in this sector. Without coming right out and saying it, Kent gave the Klingons the idea we're responsible. He says it's just a story he made up."

"If I were the suspicious type, I'd be suspicious of a claim like that."

Kirk nodded. "He may have been telling me a big story just for effect, too. We were both pretty angry. This may be a good time to ask him about it again. I might not get an answer from Starfleet for days." He glanced in Kent's direction and saw him laughing as he listened to Uhura speak. Maybe Uhura should ask the question. Kent was not the first man to be fascinated by her.

He and McCoy went over to listen to the end of Uhura's story. Kirk had heard it before. It concerned a communications officer named Eliot who mistook the claw-clackings of crustaceans on Prufrock's World for enemy code.

When Kent finished laughing Kirk said, "I'm sorry if I seemed, er, impatient this afternoon on the bridge."

"No, no, Captain. I'm the one who should apologize. I understand how nervous you must get with strangers watching you."

Kirk said, "It's not—"

McCoy interrupted, saying, "I believe you had a

question for Mr. Kent, Captain." McCoy rocked innocently on his toes.

McCoy was right, of course. Another angry scene would do none of them any good. Kirk got hold of himself and said, "Indeed I have, Doctor. Mr. Kent, this afternoon you told me the notion of a secret weapon was just a story for the Klingons, but I can't help but wonder if something more is going on."

"You wish me to answer here, Captain? Now?"

"Unless you have some reason not to answer here and now."

"Of course not. Let me only suggest that you ask Professor Omen about your suspicions."

Kirk and McCoy were both surprised by that answer. Kirk asked, "Professor Omen? The Federation scientist who led the team that developed the latest generation of starship weaponry?"

"The same."

"Why ask Omen?" Kirk asked. "Is he responsible for the disappearances?"

Kent said, "Omen is the weapons expert, isn't he? If the Federation is making Klingon ships disappear, he'd be the man who would know about it."

"Then there *is* a weapon," Kirk said.

"I didn't say that."

Kent was very annoying. Kirk said, "You're playing with me, Mr. Kent. If this thing is secret, say the word, and I'm through asking questions. If it's your own invention, we can all have a good laugh at my expense and hope that, as you insist, the Klingons can be persuaded not to believe the Federation has attacked them. But I dislike being purposely misled."

"Ask Professor Omen."

"I am not likely to run into Professor Omen out here."

"Not out here, Captain." Kent smiled. "At Starbase 12. And the Professor will have a little assignment for you."

Chapter Three

"WHAT SORT OF little assignment?" Kirk asked.

"Professor Omen will tell you."

"I don't like games, Mr. Kent."

"Then don't play them with *me,* Kirk. You've sailed under sealed orders before. You know the drill."

"My orders don't generally come from civilians with a grudge."

Kent stared at Kirk with amusement for a few seconds, and then called, "Come, Ms. Payton. I believe the reception is over."

Kent and Payton left as they had arrived, in a dramatic flurry.

Kirk paced back and forth as he watched them go. The ship was still his. He could take them back to Pegasus IV and be rid of them. He was angry enough to do that, but he was also a military man trained to take orders. In this case, of course, the orders did not come from a reliable source, and they seemed ridiculous on their face. No, the thing that prevented Kirk from taking Kent and Payton back to Pegasus IV was curiosity—about a number of things.

First of all, R and R had been cut short because Kent had specifically asked for the *Enterprise* to take him and Payton to Starbase 12. Why the *Enterprise?*

Second, Kent had spoken of a secret weapon that was eating Klingon ships and not leaving any crumbs. Did the weapon exist? Kent claimed it did not. Either way, Kent was playing a dangerous game. And if the weapon *did* exist, had it been developed by Starfleet? Had it been developed by Professor Omen? Weren't these the same thing?

Third, either Professor Omen was involved in all this somehow or Kent was just bluffing. There was no point to his bluffing—he was already en route to Starbase 12. What more could he buy by invoking the name of Professor Omen?

Kirk damned himself for his own curiosity—but he had to give Kent his due. The man had not gotten onto the Federation Council by being stupid. And Payton did not do any job without an order from Kent. Where did that leave Kirk and the *Enterprise?*

He looked around at his people. They were still drinking, talking, having a good time. He announced, "Good night, everyone. Please feel free to continue. It might be a long time before we resume our shore leave. Mr. Spock?"

Spock followed him into the corridor. As they walked toward the turbolift Kirk said, "What do you know about Professor Omen?"

"Brilliant scientist. Chief designer of the current generation of starship phasers and photon torpedoes. I believe the *Enterprise* armaments are his design."

"Very good. Anything more? Anything not in the textbooks?"

"He is something of a mystery man. To my knowledge, he has no close friends, and he's been known to disappear for months at a time without explanation."

"Mystery man, eh? Anything else?"

"Nothing but the usual biographical data. May I inquire as to why you have a sudden interest in Professor Omen?"

"Conrad Franklin Kent tells me that we will be meeting him at Starbase 12, and that he will fill us in on the secret weapon the Klingon spoke of."

"Indeed?" An eyebrow shot up.

They reached the turbolift, and Kirk said he was going to bed. The last thing he saw as the doors closed was Spock standing with his hands clasped behind his back, ruminating on what Kirk had just told him.

By the time the *Enterprise* arrived at Starbase 12 Kirk's curiosity was overshadowed by his dislike for Conrad Franklin Kent and his aide. They were always underfoot, poking, prodding, asking impolite questions. And since showing off that sensory augmenter at the famous reception, Hazel Payton wore it seemingly all the time. She recorded:

Conrad Franklin Kent in the officers' lounge contemplating the starscape outside the port.

Conrad Franklin Kent sampling coffee and doughnuts with the crew down in the mess on Deck 17.

Conrad Franklin Kent correcting various misconceptions that Chief Engineer Montgomery Scott had about warp technology.

Despite his curiosity about Professor Omen, Kirk was inclined to beam his passengers over to Starbase 12 and accelerate into warp before they were finished sparkling.

But as Sulu went through normal Starfleet arrival protocols with the starbase, Uhura received a personal message for Kirk from its commander, Commodore Favere. Favere requested the presence of Kirk and his first officer at their earliest convenience so that they might discuss a matter of grave importance.

Kirk didn't know Favere and so didn't know his definition of "grave importance." But to ignore such an invitation was impolite at the very least, and at worst it could deprive Kirk of important information that Starfleet might not get around to telling him for months. The *Enterprise* was a long way out, and Starfleet had other things on its collective mind. Besides, a meeting with a new face was a novelty that neither starship captains nor starbase commanders enjoyed every day.

Kirk said, "Uhura, inform the commodore that Mr. Spock and I would be delighted to meet with him even if we don't discuss matters of 'grave importance.'"

"Aye, sir."

The official good-byes between Kirk and his passengers were rather stiff, but altogether heartfelt. It seemed to Kirk that Kent still kept secrets that would have been of interest; but at this point Kirk knew that asking would gain him nothing, and he refused to give

Kent the pleasure of being evasive. He sighed as they disappeared at last.

Commodore Favere met Kent and Payton in the starbase's transporter room.

"Good to see you again, sir," Favere said as the two of them shook hands.

"I'm certain that's not true, Commodore, but it's nice of you to say so." He glanced at Payton and said, "You and Ms. Payton probably have a lot to discuss. If you'll have a yeoman show me to my quarters, I'll leave you two alone."

"Yes, sir," Favere said with astonishment. He motioned for a yeoman, who stepped forward and asked Kent to follow him. Favere and Payton watched them go, and then Favere said, "This way, Ms. Payton." Payton tried to suppress a smile.

He picked up her duffel and led her through Starbase 12. When they arrived at Favere's office and the door shushed closed he dropped her duffel and engulfed Payton in a thorough kiss. She wrapped her arms around him, and for many moments the only noise in the room—other than the constant and forgotten hiss of the air conditioning—was that of heavy breathing.

They stopped kissing, though the clinch continued, and Favere said, "Knowing how he feels about Starfleet in general and about our relationship in particular, I'm surprised that Mr. Kent left us alone without a fight."

"Actually, he likes you," Payton said. "He just considers you a nice man who's been misled into a bad career."

"My family has been in one service or another for generations."

"Exactly. Misled." She broke away from him gently and walked around the room, touching the three-horned skull, the yellow braid of a blue uniform displayed on a dummy, the back of Favere's chair.

Favere smiled wistfully as he watched her. He said, "It's been over a year."

"I would have expected you to be married to some Orion slave girl by now."

"Not much chance for that sort of thing way out here."

She sat down in his chair and made it swivel up and back as she swung her knees. She said, "So, is Professor Omen here?"

"He is, and he gives me the creeps."

"We could have saved your nerves and held the test somewhere else."

"You could have," Favere admitted.

They both smiled fondly.

Favere sat down in the chair before the desk and said, "Seriously, Hazel, I don't like him."

"He's smarter than almost everybody. That's bound to make a man difficult."

"Have you met him?"

"No."

"You'll see what I mean. I also don't understand why you needed the *Enterprise* for the test. The flagship of the fleet, after all."

Payton pursed her lips and thought for a moment. "What if I asked you to trust me on that?"

Favere shrugged and said, "I suppose I'd trust you." He shook his head. "Still, with everything so carefully arranged, to have Kent, and Omen, and the *Enterprise* all here at the same time, I can't help wondering if it's something I should know officially."

Payton looked at the desk, and then up at Favere in a suggestive way. She said, "There must be something we can talk about besides Starfleet business and Federation politics."

Favere's face reddened.

"What?" asked Payton.

He came around to her side of the desk and opened a drawer. From within he took a small velvet box. Payton sat very still and watched him solemnly. Favere opened the box to reveal a jeweled ring that sparkled like fire, even in the indirect office lighting.

"Marry me," said Favere.

Payton said nothing. She did not move. She barely breathed.

"You don't love me," Favere said.

"I do," said Payton, "but I have to consider Mr. Kent. I don't think he'd approve."

"You don't need his approval," Favere said angrily. "He's your boss, not your father. And even if he were your father, you're old enough to make your own decisions. Marry me."

Payton stood and slowly went to the other side of the desk, where she put her fingertips on the top and turned her head as if she were alternately taking opposite sides in an argument. At last she said, "He's been like a father to me. He saw something in me no one else did and gave me opportunities that I could not have dreamed of if I'd stayed in school. He's advised me and taken care of me. Sometimes I did the same for him. I would hate to hurt him."

"It's *your* life," Favere said.

"Yes," Payton agreed. "I'll think it over."

Favere nodded. She waited for more: more conversation, more kissing, more attention. When he did notice her again he said, "You'd better go. I have a meeting with Kirk and his first officer in a few minutes. You're on Deck 3, Cabin 37."

"I really will think it over," Payton said.

Favere nodded again. When Payton went out he sat down in his chair and, with finality, shut the boxed ring back in the drawer. He picked up an empty rifle shell and tossed it in his hand.

After completing administrative details connected with docking at a starbase, Kirk left the bridge to Scotty and beamed over to Starbase 12 with Mr. Spock.

As was the case with many starbases, this one had taken on the personality of the person in charge, and that personality now overlaid the utilitarian Starfleet designs. Hanging at intervals in every corridor were mementos of the nineteenth-century (old calendar) American Wild West. There were paintings of horse soldiers dealing with Native Americans, feathered drums, headdresses many feet long, crossed lances, and framed proclamations announcing the forced movement of various Native American tribes from one part of the old United States to another.

Favere's office had the same flavor as his starbase, but more so. He had on display various cavalry uniforms, spurs, buttons, insignia, braid, pistols, and crossed sabers. In one corner a saddle was slung across what appeared to be a wooden hitching rail. On the corner of his desk was an animal skull; but unlike earthly cattle, it had three horns. Behind him, next to a rack of highly polished rifles, was a poster advertising someone named John Wayne in a production called *She Wore a Yellow Ribbon*. Favere himself was a slim, muscular man, somewhat older than Kirk, with close-cropped blond hair. He drawled in a folksy way that reminded Kirk of McCoy at his most ingenuous.

As they shook hands Kirk looked around appreciatively and said, "You seem fascinated by the old United States Cavalry."

"Not the cavalry so much as the system of forts that sprang up across the west after the American Civil War."

"Not a happy time for the inhabitants of North America," said Mr. Spock. "Particularly not for the native inhabitants."

"It was a time of courage and cowardice, of great deeds and some deeds so despicable as to be embarrassing for humankind even today."

"It was a time of life and death," said Kirk. "Like any time."

"My point exactly. Today's starbases serve the same purpose as the forts of the old west. We represent Federation civilization to colonists and to enemies alike. We survey. We put out diplomatic and military brush fires. In short, we are the 'law west of the Pecos.'"

"A colorful if not wholly accurate description," said Spock.

Kirk could see that Favere was ready to talk for

hours about the nineteenth-century cavalry, and though Kirk was amenable, North American history could hardly be the matter of grave importance that had drawn them there in the first place.

When Kirk mentioned this, Favere smiled shyly and said, "You're right, Captain. I am always comfortable riding my hobby horse, and I occasionally lose track of time." He put down the empty rifle cartridge he'd been rolling around in his fingers and said, "Something inexplicable is happening in this sector, and it is reaching epidemic proportions."

Kirk said, "Klingon ships are disappearing without a trace."

"Not just Klingons," Favere replied. "Romulans, and even Federation ships. But how did you know?"

"We encountered a disgruntled Klingon on our way here."

Spock said, "Earlier we had surmised that a Federation weapon was responsible. Apparently that is not the case."

"Apparently," Kirk said. So Kent had been bluffing after all. If the Federation diplomats could prove to the Klingons' satisfaction that Starfleet ships were disappearing as well as Klingon ships, perhaps war could be avoided, despite Kent's bluff. Then what was all this business about Professor Omen?

"Have a look at this," Favere said. He handed Kirk a memoboard on which page one already appeared. The report told essentially the same story that Torm of the *Kormak* had told, though in more polite language. It took several pages for the report to say that ships were disappearing without a trace. They didn't have time to radio a distress call back to base or to drop a marker buoy. No wreckage, not even molecular or energy traces remained—not that anyone could find, anyway.

Kirk handed the memoboard to Spock and asked Favere, "What's being done about this?"

"Not much so far. Starfleet has sent out a few scout ships—that's how we got all this negative information —but aside from that, nobody knew what to do except be outraged. Till now."

"Till now?" Kirk asked. He believed he knew on what plan of action Starfleet had settled. It was inevitable.

"Yesterday I received a subspace communiqué from Starfleet Command, Priority One and scrambled."

Spock looked up from the memoboard and said, "Excuse me, Commodore, but no doubt you have noticed the single critical piece of information this report *does* contain."

"What is it, Spock?" Kirk asked.

"We know very little about the Klingon or Romulan fleets, of course, but if the Starfleet disappearances continue at their present rate, the Federation will be without a fleet in less than two solar years."

Spock spoke this shocking news calmly. Knowing Spock as he did, Kirk would have been surprised if he'd done anything else. But apparently Favere had little experience with Vulcans.

"Doesn't that bother you, Mr. Spock?" Favere asked.

"I am a Vulcan," Spock said. "Facts neither bother nor elate me. They simply are. Still, I admit that it would be prudent to take action to prevent the piece-meal destruction of Starfleet."

Kirk said, "Maybe the Starfleet communiqué will suggest what that action might be." With a sense of inevitability Kirk took the chip from Favere and inserted it into the top of the board. He punched in his code, and the scrambled message straightened itself out. Though he'd not known what the specifics of the message would be, he'd correctly guessed its general outline. It excited him. He swallowed and said, "They're sending the *Enterprise* to find out what's going on and to stop it. They don't even say 'if possible.' Just 'stop it.' " He smiled philosophically and said, "We never get the easy ones, do we, Spock?"

Spock shrugged and said, "It does seem that our reputation precedes us."

"The order says that we'll be taking Professor Omen with us. Starfleet thinks his experience with weapons design will be helpful. Is Professor Omen here?"

"He is," Favere said.

Kirk said, "At least Kent didn't lie about that." He stood up and said, "Good. Then we can leave immediately." Kirk was pleased that the mystery had been cleared up at last. Though *why* Kent insisted that it be a mystery, Kirk did not know. Maybe it was just another example of the suspicious political mind in action.

Favere said, "I'm afraid that's not possible. Professor Omen's test is tomorrow."

"Test?" Kirk asked. "What test?"

Favere looked uncomfortable. "Mr. Kent didn't tell you?"

"Mr. Kent told us very little that was of any use," Spock said.

Favere said, "Omen has developed a new phased shield generator."

"Phased?" Spock asked. His eyebrows were up. Kirk knew that this was the Vulcan equivalent of showing wild curiosity.

"Yes, phased," Favere said. "Though I don't pretend to understand it myself."

"If I know Kent," Kirk said with disgust, "the *Enterprise* is probably the target."

"No, we have an old freighter for that. The *Enterprise* is going to be the aggressor."

Kirk nodded. The need for the *Enterprise* to be at Starbase 12 was now clear. Starfleet was killing two birds with one stone—testing the new generators and having the *Enterprise* available to take Omen out to solve the problem of the disappearing ships. Then something else occurred to Kirk. He said, "But why here? Why Starbase 12?"

"Well," said Favere, "there's the matter of secrecy, of course. It's much easier to keep something secret out here."

"Secrecy, of course," Spock said.

"And there's Hazel."

"Hazel?" asked Kirk.

"Ms. Payton. Mr. Kent's aide. She and I are, uh, very close. We hadn't seen each other for a long time. We thought that Starbase 12 would do for the site of the test as well as anywhere else, and she pulled a few strings."

With some embarrassment Kirk remembered the play he'd made for Hazel Payton. Knowing what he knew now, he was glad he hadn't completed his pass. Knowing what he knew now, he was certain that completing it would have been impossible.

Spock said, "Excuse me, Commodore, but there is one thing I still do not understand. The *Enterprise* and Omen are here both for the test and to study the problem of the disappearing starships. Though I can appreciate your pleasure at Ms. Payton's presence, Mr. Kent's interest in this is still unknown. Is he here for Ms. Payton's benefit, or for some other, more personal reason? It seems unlikely that Starfleet would approve of a Federation Council observer who is so unfriendly."

Favere said, "My feelings exactly, Mr. Spock. I have a hunch that something else is going on. But I have not yet been able to find out what it is."

"I am familiar with the concept of hunches, Commodore. And while I believe intuition to be an unreliable resource at best, I have learned that some humans can draw surprisingly accurate conclusions from surprisingly little data."

Kirk said, "Call it what you will, Mr. Spock. I have a bad feeling about all this myself."

Chapter Four

Kirk received his orders for the test. They were simple enough. He was to fire everything the *Enterprise* had at a gutted old class-J freighter protected only by a deflector erected by one of Professor Omen's phased field generators. If the freighter was still there when the *Enterprise* was finished, the test would be declared a success. The fireworks had been the talk of Starbase 12 for weeks. Kirk could not help being irritated that these people had known about the test before he had. Surely Kent could have told him.

Spock spent a few hours reading everything in the memory banks of both the *Enterprise* and Starbase 12 concerning conventional force fields and phased force fields. He told Kirk, "There was considerably more information on the former than on the latter. Thus far, the strength of shields has been limited by the strength of materials used to build their generators, and we seem to have reached the theoretical limit. If Professor Omen has succeeded in raising that limit by phasing the field, then he has made yet another breakthrough. I will look forward to discussing it with him at dinner this evening."

Kirk himself was ambivalent about attending the dinner. As a matter of fact, when the invitation had come from Commodore Favere, Kirk had even considered declining. Kirk had no interest in eating with Conrad Franklin Kent ever again. But he had a few questions for Kent, and the dinner would give him an opportunity to ask them. Besides, Professor Omen was sure to be there, and one way or another, *that* was sure to be interesting—at least until he and Spock climbed into a mathematical stratosphere where few could follow.

As McCoy joined Kirk and Spock on the transporter stage he pulled at the collar of his formal Starfleet uniform and said, "I don't know why you always drag me into these diplomatic affairs."

"Why should I suffer alone?" Kirk asked.

McCoy and Spock traded dubious expressions. McCoy said, "I was about to mention that you already had Spock, but then I remembered that Spock likes to keep his suffering to himself."

"Right. He's no fun. Besides, you have to eat anyway." He nodded at Mr. Kyle and said, "Energize."

People gathered in a room that was rather bare by Starbase 12 standards. Everything was contemporary, and colored the usual Starfleet gray, red, or black.

Favere was in one corner of the room with Kent and Payton. Even if he had not known that Favere was in love with Payton, Kirk would have guessed. No one could fail to notice the way Favere leaned close when she spoke, laughed at her jokes, and rarely took his eyes off her.

Payton was wearing her sensory augmenter, which made Kirk a little nervous. He was certain that few other people at the event knew what the fancy jewelry in Payton's hair was, which struck Kirk as taking unfair advantage, but chances were good that nothing much would happen that evening that would be of general interest. The recording would probably be buried in Kent's archives. Besides, Kirk liked to choose his battles. He had other things he wanted to argue about with Kent.

"Which one is Omen?" McCoy asked.

"The available holos are very old, but I believe I would recognize him even so. He has not yet arrived."

"Big disappointment, eh, Spock?"

"No, Doctor. My only concern is that I have lost an opportunity to speak with someone whose every statement is not a childish emotional outburst."

McCoy said, "I can be witty if there's anybody around to appreciate it."

Kirk said, "You can fight on the ship, gentlemen. Let's mingle." He grabbed a drink from an automated tray that floated by and headed for Kent. Kirk could see no point putting off their discussion. Before he made it to the other side of the room, however, a man dressed in a cavalry uniform opened double doors and announced that dinner was served.

Immediately the crowd drifted toward the doors

and into the room beyond. The officer's mess was decorated in much the same way as the rest of the starbase. Cavalry flags hung in shreds from the front wall. Kirk assumed they were simulations of flags that had been through battles.

Kirk found his name card and sat down. Under his name were the printed words, "This dinner catered for your enjoyment by Enyart's, famous for fine dining across the galaxy." Kirk should have guessed that Enyart's would be called in. Favere would want to impress his very important guests, and Enyart's always put on a good feed. No matter what else happened, dinner would be worth eating.

A pretty redheaded lieutenant sat down on one side of him, and an elderly civilian woman sat down on the other. The civilian put out her hand and said, "I'm Dr. Kroeber. You must be Captain Kirk of the *Enterprise.*" She leaned across Kirk and whispered to the lieutenant in a voice loud enough to carry to the entire table, "Be careful of this one, dear. He's much too charming for either your good or his."

The lieutenant looked at the old woman in amazement and then was distracted by McCoy, who, with obvious delight, sat on her other side. He glanced a second time at his name card and nodded with approval.

"I don't know whether to be flattered or not," Kirk said to Dr. Kroeber.

"That's all right, dear," she said. "I don't know how I meant it."

Kirk liked Dr. Kroeber immediately and found himself talking to her more than to the lieutenant, whose name was Goshalk. McCoy made sure that

Goshalk didn't feel lonely. Kirk watched the women on either side of Spock try to chat with him, but with little success. Spock was unfailingly polite and could hold forth on a variety of subjects, but on the whole he was more geared for the classroom than for the dinner party.

Kirk bowed his head to listen to a *very* off-color story that Dr. Kroeber told with some gusto. When she came to the improbable punchline and Kirk lifted his head to laugh, he saw that sitting directly across from him was Conrad Franklin Kent. Suddenly Kirk did not feel like laughing. He and Kent nodded civilly at each other, but before Kirk had a chance to ask any questions yeomen appeared with heaping trays of food. Kirk grumbled.

Kirk took a slab of meat and a spoonful each of the side dishes. He found the flavor of the meat to be delicious but heavy and quite unusual. He guessed it had come from some non-sapient alien species, but when someone farther down the table asked what it was, Favere said it was buffalo. "Not real buffalo, of course, but a very good simulacrum made by the Enyart's food replicators. I have no idea where they got the program."

Many people at the table did not know what a buffalo was, and Favere took pleasure in explaining. Then he pointed to the various dishes and told what they were. It seemed that most of them were made of corn—replicator corn, anyway—although some were made from native North American plants that Kirk had never heard of. Though he did not eat meat, between the side dishes and the salad, Spock would not go hungry.

For a long time the only sounds Kirk heard were the sharp taps of utensils against crockery. Various people mentioned that Professor Omen had not yet appeared.

"As a matter of fact," Dr. Kroeber said, "I have never spoken with *anyone* who's seen him."

"Human question mark, eh?" Kirk asked.

"Apparently. His staff must talk with him, of course. I meant besides them. And the mystery seems to have rubbed off." She looked up and down the table. "None of Omen's staff are here either. Maybe they're installing the field generator in the freighter, but I doubt it." She sipped her wine and said, "We'll be lucky if he comes out for his own test."

Kirk glanced down the table and saw a female lieutenant with big doe eyes hanging on Spock's every well-considered word. It was amazing. The less interest Spock showed in women, the more intrigued they became. His line of devotees did not end with McCoy's Nurse Chapel.

"Enjoying your dinner, Mr. Kent?" Dr. Kroeber asked.

"Very much so," Kent said. "North American history has always been an interest of mine. It seems appropriate that we eat this kind of food way out here on the Federation frontier."

"Looking forward to the big test, sir?" a freckle-faced command ensign asked.

Kirk was about to answer when Kent said, "Indeed I am. But with some trepidation, I might add."

"Why is that, sir?"

Before he answered, Kent carefully spread a spoonful of corn relish over what remained of his buffalo steak. He pointed at the ensign with the empty spoon and said, "I believe that we in the Federation will lose no matter what the outcome of the test."

"How's that?" Dr. Kroeber asked.

"Well, if the phased shield generators don't work, an important Federation scientist will have wasted months of his time. If it does work, then Starfleet will have a bigger shield to hide behind."

In the sudden silence McCoy coughed and appraised Kirk. Many of the diners did the same, and Kirk knew why. As the ranking officer within earshot of Kent's slander, he was obligated to defend Starfleet. Was it Kent's intention to drag him into an argument? Kirk decided that Kent's intentions didn't matter. He said, "I don't follow you, Councilman."

"I meant only this: With a deflector of this strength, Starfleet will feel confident to go into battle more often, to take even greater risks with its crews and equipment."

McCoy made an impolite "Hah."

"What Dr. McCoy means to say," Kirk said in a reasonable tone, "is that Starfleet has always been more interested in peace than in war. And a shield is not an offensive weapon. It is not a weapon at all."

"Not in the conventional sense, no," Kent admitted.

Kirk chuckled and touched his lips with his napkin. He said, "If you are convinced we lose either way, I can't help but wonder why you're wasting your time out here on the, ah, Federation frontier at all, sir."

"I have my reasons, sir," Kent said.

"Secret reasons?"

"Secret Federation reasons."

"That's convenient," McCoy grumbled.

Innocently Kirk said, "I suppose those secret reasons also cover that *other* weapon Professor Omen is said to be working on. The one we discussed aboard the *Enterprise?* Professor Omen doesn't seem to be here to speak for himself."

"This is hardly the place for such a discussion, Captain, as you well know."

"Perhaps later—"

"Perhaps you should wait to speak with Professor Omen about that. He is sure to be at the test tomorrow."

He'd made Kent sweat a little, which was all Kirk had intended to do. A weapon of such power should not be discussed before a group of this size, if there was really anything to discuss. Kirk said, "I will look forward to the opportunity."

Even if Omen did show up at the test, Kirk thought it unlikely that he would be able to clear up anything. Starfleet wouldn't be sending him out with the *Enterprise* if they already knew what was going on. And a weapons expert might be no help to them anyway; Kent was still denying that a weapon existed, after all. That left them with a lot of missing starships. Unless Kent and Omen had gone into business for themselves, Kirk doubted that either of them would snipe at Federation ships.

Which left Kirk with either a brace of traitors or a mystery. Kirk could hardly accuse Kent of treason based on the evidence he had in hand. And Kirk had even less evidence against Omen. All Kirk could do was stay awake and be ready to drop a noose if the proper neck presented itself.

Dessert came—ice cream with chocolate sauce—and Favere assured everyone that this was the only part of the meal that was not authentic to the nineteenth-century North American west. "However, ice cream and chocolate sauce is a particular favorite of one of my favorite people." He looked at Payton and she blushed.

After dessert people lingered over coffee and tea. Lieutenant Goshalk asked to see Dr. Kroeber alone for a moment. As Lieutenant Goshalk went out the door Dr. Kroeber explained to Kirk, "She's having some trouble with her young man. I've been coaching her."

"Her young man?" McCoy asked.

"I'm very sorry, Doctor," Dr. Kroeber said, and she patted his arm as she followed Lieutenant Goshalk.

McCoy stretched and said, "I've had enough disappointment for one evening. What about you, Jim?"

"I have some unfinished business."

McCoy glanced at Kent, who was speaking to a yeoman as he poured more coffee. McCoy leaned across the empty chair between them and whispered to Kirk, "I don't want to see you in sickbay with a bloody nose. Not tonight, anyway."

"I wouldn't think of disturbing your beauty sleep, Bones."

McCoy and the Captain said their good nights, and McCoy walked carefully away.

As he sipped his coffee Kent watched Payton and Favere through narrow eyes. At last Kirk got tired of waiting for Kent to finish and went into the reception room where crowds had gathered to say extended good nights. Many people wished Kirk well on the test tomorrow, as if his invention were on the line instead of Professor Omen's.

As the evening got later Kirk felt increasingly heavy, both physically and mentally. Through layers of fatigue and indulgence he was debating whether he really wanted yet another confrontation with Kent when Kent wandered into the reception room with a group of civilians.

"Good night, Kirk," Kent said as he lifted his hand in a desultory wave.

Kirk asked, "Can I speak with you, Mr. Kent?"

"Tonight?"

"No time like the present."

Kent looked around at the people he was with, asked to be excused, and walked with Kirk into the corridor.

Kirk said, "I have reason to believe that Professor Omen knows nothing about the disappearances."

Kent rubbed his eyes as he said, "What reasons are those, Captain?"

"We all have our secrets, Councilman. I'm sure you understand."

Kent thought for a moment before he said, "He's the weapons expert."

"You said there wasn't a weapon."

"No Federation weapon."

They held each other's stare until Mr. Spock came by with his doe-eyed lieutenant. She had wrapped herself around Spock's arm. He appeared to be uncomfortable, yet he was not struggling. Spock was, as Kirk noted before, unfailingly polite.

"Why, Mr. Spock," Kirk said with some glee.

"Good evening, Captain. Lieutenant Clark insisted that I escort her home."

"Of course."

"Good night, Captain, Mr. Kent."

"Good night," Kent and Kirk said together.

After they were gone Kent said, "Look, Kirk, we each have our reasons for believing what we do, and that's fine. But believe me when I tell you this: If Professor Omen can't tell you what's going on, then nobody can. Good night."

Kent wandered off looking like no more than a man on the verge of old age going home too late from a party. He seemed harmless, like a man who really knew as little as he claimed. Still, Kirk did not trust him; he had no reason to. Kirk rubbed his own eyes. They felt as if they did not quite fit their sockets. It was late. He was thinking in circles. And the next day he had to attack a gutted class-J freighter. Big job. It really needed the flagship of the fleet. Kirk shook his head as he walked to the transporter, short one bloody nose.

McCoy would be pleased that he was not disturbed.

Kirk was not at his best the following morning; he rarely was the morning after a party. But he'd felt worse, and fortunately *Enterprise* time and Starbase 12 time were within two hours of each other, so warp lag was not much of a problem. The test was to take place at ten hundred hours local time. Kirk lingered over a light breakfast and then went up to the bridge.

Status reports came in from all over the ship. Uhura was speaking to Starbase 12 control, and Spock was giving orders to a yeoman who was concentrating very hard to keep track of them. On the main viewscreen, under a tactical overlay, was the awkward fishlike bulk of the class-J freighter. Sulu and Chekov were checking the weapons systems, recalibrating when necessary. Watching over Sulu's shoulder was a blond civilian female dressed in a simple blue jumpsuit. The serious expression on her handsome face only added to her charm.

Kirk walked up to McCoy, who was sitting in the command chair. "Comfy?" Kirk asked.

"Oh, sorry, Captain," McCoy said as he stood and stepped down to stand next to the chair. "Not much happening in sickbay, so I thought I'd come up to see the fireworks. This was the only vacant chair."

"That's all right, Bones, just don't get used to it. Mr. Sulu, perhaps you would introduce me to your friend."

"Yes, sir. This is Bahia Slocum. She's here observing for Professor Omen."

With some surprise Kirk asked, "The professor himself won't be joining us?"

Slocum said, "The professor has much to do. He can't be everywhere at once."

"Of course. Please continue, Mr. Sulu. Status, Mr. Spock."

"We are running diagnostics on all systems, Captain, and sensors are in full-record mode. At last report we were within five percent of Starfleet specifications."

"Very good. What is our time?"

"Fifteen minutes, seventeen seconds and counting."

"Very good."

Kirk immersed himself in the brisk activity around him, and the fifteen minutes passed quickly. As they approached ten hundred hours Spock began a verbal countdown.

"Message coming in for Ms. Slocum," Uhura said. "Audio only."

"Ms. Slocum, if you would care for some privacy—"

"No, Captain. It's Omen with his final check."

"Very well, Ms. Slocum. Let's hear it, Lieutenant."

"Aye, Captain."

Uhura opened a channel, and a voice said, "Bahia, are you there?" It was a cultured voice; overcultured, Kirk decided, deep, resonant, trained. It thought a lot of itself, and yet, as it spoke to Bahia Slocum, it was not unkind. Ultimately the voice told Kirk little more about Professor Omen than would a Starfleet press release.

Slocum said, "Here, sir."

"Weapons?"

"Go/no-go tests satisfactorily completed. Photon torpedoes are armed and ready. Phasers are fully charged."

"Weapons systems?"

"I am in constant communication with Chief Engineer Scott. He and Ensign Chekov assure me that targeting and launch systems are calibrated and ready. As are all primary and secondary guidance and feedback systems."

"Firing program?"

"Sequencers are programmed and ready. Automatic firing will commence on your command."

"Sensors?"

"Ready," said Mr. Spock.

Slocum looked at him and said, "Ready, sir. We won't miss a thing."

"Very well. At my mark we are at three minutes, fourteen seconds and counting. Mark. Omen out."

Slocum backed away from Sulu and joined McCoy next to the center seat. She studied him for a moment and said, "I assume you're cleared for this area."

McCoy seemed surprised at the question, but he answered politely enough. "I think you can safely do that." He looked at the captain for confirmation. Kirk nodded with a straight face.

Spock gave them a count every ten seconds down to thirty seconds and counting, and every second thereafter. At ten seconds and counting Omen's voice filled the bridge again. "You may fire when ready, Captain."

"Thank you, Professor."

At five seconds and counting Kirk said, "Mr. Chekov, you may fire when ready."

"Aye, Captain."

At the stroke of ten hundred hours Chekov touched a single control, and Kirk heard the peculiar electronic sneeze of a launching photon torpedo. Then again and again. The *Enterprise* shuddered with the force of their leaving. The fan of torpedoes converged on the freighter and exploded with a light so bright it could almost be felt as well as seen.

"Sequencing program holding fire," Chekov said.

"Spock?" Kirk asked.

"Sensors report that both shield and hull integrity remain. Freighter shield strength fell by two percent during attack."

"This is well within design parameters," Slocum said.

"Very well. Mr. Chekov, continue."

"Aye, Captain."

A spray of phaser fire spread against the freighter. Where the incandescent beams touched the shield Kirk could actually see it blush red, as if a forge were behind it. As the attack continued and more power was poured into the phasers the red brightened into orange, and then up the spectrum: yellow, green, blue, indigo, and then into a violet that grew in intensity until the freighter looked like a tiny white sun. Beams reflected away at odd angles. Then even the white light was replaced by a black smudge that blotted out a freighter-shaped section of stars.

"Spock?"

"Shields now at maximum, radiating in the ultraviolet, but withstanding attack. They are reflecting what they cannot absorb. Shield and hull integrity continue. Interior temperature of freighter is well within normal life-support limits."

"Ten seconds remain," Chekov said. He counted down to zero, and the phaser banks cut off. Suddenly everything was quiet. The bridge, which for the last few minutes had been filled with bright light, now looked dingy under its normal illumination.

"Shield and hull integrity remain," Spock said. "Life support conditions inside the freighter remain nominal."

"We did it," Slocum cried. She shook McCoy's hand vigorously.

"Congratulations, Ms. Slocum," Kirk said.

"Indeed," said Spock. "Very impressive. I would

like very much to speak to Professor Omen about his discovery."

"I suspect you're not alone, Spock. I'm sure your moment will come."

"Aye, Captain."

Kirk and Spock both knew that Omen would be setting off with them the next day to search for the thing eating starships. Chances were very good that Spock would be one of the few aboard the *Enterprise* who would be competent to converse with Omen on technical matters.

Slocum said, "I must go, Captain. Omen will want to go over the test results with a fine-toothed comb."

"Don't let me stop you, Ms. Slocum. Please extend the congratulations of the *Enterprise* to Professor Omen."

"Thank you, Captain." She rushed out.

"Uhura, see that the Starbase 12 computer gets full sensor readouts of the test. Spock, prepare for departure tomorrow at oh-nine-hundred hours, ship's time."

"Aye, Captain."

Uhura said, "Captain, message coming in from Councilman Kent."

"Tell him we're busy, Lieutenant."

"I tried that, sir. He is most insistent."

"Maybe he just wants to say good-bye," McCoy whispered.

Kirk smiled and said, "On screen, Lieutenant."

Kent, looking exhilarated, replaced the freighter. He said, "Congratulations, Kirk."

"Sarcasm, Mr. Kent?"

"Not at all, Kirk. Whatever I may think of the political ramifications, the fact that the phased shield works is a stunning technical achievement."

Kirk considered reminding Kent that he'd had nothing to do with developing the shield, but there was no point. Kent was a politician—he was making political noises. Kirk merely said, "Thank you, Mr. Kent."

"Yes. And to celebrate this event I'd like you, Mr. Spock, and Dr. McCoy to join me in my cabin for a drink."

Kirk took a moment to look at Spock. He knew that Spock was wondering if Omen would be there. Kirk normally did not mind satisfying Spock's curiosity, but in this case Spock could wait. They would be seeing a lot of Omen in the next few weeks. Besides, Kirk tried not to accept drinking invitations from people he didn't like. It was bad for the soul. He said, "I'm afraid that isn't possible, Mr. Kent. The *Enterprise* is leaving with the tide tomorrow morning on a mission of the greatest importance. My crew and I have much to do before we cast off."

"The tide?"

"Just a figure of speech. The fact remains that we have no time for victory drinks."

"I assure you, Captain, ignoring me will not help Starfleet's cause."

"Mr. Kent, if my drinking with you will change your mind about Starfleet, I mistook the depth of your convictions. Kirk out." He made the cutthroat sign to Uhura, and the freighter returned to the main viewscreen.

McCoy said, "It's satisfying not to suffer fools gladly, isn't it, Jim?"

"He's no fool, Bones. But it was satisfying just the same."

Kirk's sense of satisfaction lasted till after lunch. He was in his cabin reading all he could about the sector of space they'd be patrolling; it was all he could do. He couldn't prepare to meet the mystery weapon because he knew nothing about it. Uhura called and told him that three messages had just arrived.

The first was an answer to his query about the weapon. Starfleet suggested he get in touch with Commodore Favere at Starbase 12. Kirk shrugged.

The second was a personal message from Admiral Nogura once again asking—in a way that was nearly an order, but not quite—that Kirk cooperate with Conrad Franklin Kent in any way possible. Kirk wondered if Nogura had ever met the man, then he decided that what Nogura felt about Kent didn't matter. An admiral was part diplomat and part politician, as well as part Starfleet officer. Nogura probably just reasoned that cooperating with Kent would be good for the cause. Maybe he was right, but Kirk didn't have to like it.

The third message was the one Kirk liked least. Obviously Kent had told someone that Kirk wasn't cooperating, not even to the extent of drinking with him. Word had gotten to Nogura, and Nogura had assured Kent that cooperation would be forthcoming —hence the second message. The third message was an invitation to dinner from Kent. "And please bring Mr. Spock and Dr. McCoy. I have the feeling that they are confidants of yours, and they ought to be here."

Kirk disliked taking orders from civilians, even when the orders were couched in the form of an invitation, especially when he didn't like the civilian doing the inviting. But he could see no way out. Maybe they would meet Omen at last. That would be something, anyway.

Chapter Five

KIRK DECIDED not to wear his dress uniform. Kent's little party could hardly be construed as an official function. Within the narrow parameters of Nogura's order, Kirk wanted to use all the maneuvering room available to him.

As he entered the transporter room McCoy said, "I have things to do, Jim. I can't be beaming all over creation every time some muck-a-muck decides to throw a weenie roast."

"I know, Doctor. Mr. Spock said the same thing."

"He said that *I* have things to do?"

"I merely pointed out, Doctor, that participating in yet another dinner party did not make the best use of our time."

"Gentlemen, I agree with you entirely. But Starfleet

Command gives us no alternative. We will go. We will eat. We will leave as soon as we can."

They transported over to Starbase 12 and found out from the officer of the day where Kent's cabin was. Compared to the lodgings on the *Enterprise,* it was very posh. He even had a separate dining room and a separate bedroom. A fresh, hot smell filled the place. Kirk recognized it as Rigellian husk, the large bell-shaped seed of the whispering smith. Kirk had never been partial to it, but he could choke it down if he had to.

"Where's Ms. Payton?" McCoy asked.

"Out somewhere with Commodore Favere." Kent shook his head.

"Favere is an honorable Starfleet officer," Spock said.

"Exactly," Kent said, as if being a Starfleet officer were a shifty occupation.

"I'm surprised she isn't here to record our meeting for posterity," Kirk said.

"You have a bad opinion of me, Captain. But I assure you that not every waking moment is recorded."

"Editing an entire life *would* be a problem," Spock said. "For one thing, it would take another entire life just to play it back."

"Quite right, Mr. Spock," said Kent as he ushered them into the dining room. "And I, for one, have only one life."

"Are you expecting no one else for dinner?" Spock asked.

"Professor Omen sends his regrets."

Kirk noted that sometimes it paid to be a civilian, but he did not make this comment out loud. McCoy nodded. Perhaps he was thinking the same thing.

The table was beautifully set, not the rustic affair that the commodore favored. In the middle of the table was the Rigellian husk, a seed big enough to feed four easily.

"I hope you enjoy this, Mr. Spock. It is one of the few vegetarian main courses I prepare well."

"You made this yourself?" McCoy asked.

"The ability to butt heads with Starfleet is not my only talent. Please sit down." Kent poured the wine (Spock had water) and passed around the husk. Each of them took a small pod from inside the husk, tore it open, and carved the gray flesh into slices. Spock complimented Kent's cooking. Kirk would never understand Vulcan taste buds.

After they ate in silence for a while, Kent said, "I suppose, Captain, that you have a plan for discovering what happened to the missing starships."

Startled, Kirk said, "Why would I have a plan for that?"

"Starfleet always has a plan, even if it is a bad one."

"I don't know what you're talking about."

"Come, come, Captain. I deal in information. I know for a fact that Klingon ships are not the only ones disappearing. Federation and Romulan starships have disappeared as well. The *Enterprise* has been ordered to investigate the mystery."

"A lucky guess," McCoy said.

Kirk knew it was no guess. The fact that Kent had a pipeline to Starfleet Command angered Kirk. Evidently information in the pipeline flowed both ways.

"Not at all, Doctor," Spock said. "Given the situation and the presence of both the *Enterprise* and Professor Omen, it is a logical inference."

While trying to remain calm Kirk said, "Then you know we are not dealing with a Starfleet weapon."

"Of course."

Spock said, "You seemed reluctant to admit that before."

"You had not yet been given your orders."

"I see," said Kirk.

"And your plan is?"

"Classified."

Spock was about to speak and then thought better of it.

"Come, come, Kirk," said Kent.

"Come, come, Mr. Kent. You have kept secrets, used every means at your command to push me, prod me, and harass me, and all because you don't like Starfleet. Well, the fact is that Starfleet doesn't like you very much either. For that reason and for many others, both official and unofficial, my plan will stay classified."

"Bravo," said McCoy. He saluted Kirk with his glass and drank down the wine. Spock, as usual, was unperturbed. But the raised eyebrow did indicate his disapproval of Kirk's outburst.

Kent seemed surprised but not upset. Maybe it was what Kent had been angling for all along, an excuse to give Kirk trouble. Now he had it. One did not speak that way to a council member with impunity. Kirk stood and said, "We'll be going now, Councilman. Thank you for an educational evening."

McCoy and Spock stood. They moved to follow

Kirk, who was halfway to the door before Kent stopped all three of them. "I appreciate honesty, Captain, even when I am the unhappy recipient."

Kirk turned and said, "That changes nothing."

"It should. It means you will not be court-martialed. In exchange for that small favor, I have a favor to ask of you."

Kirk could not help smiling. He said, "Your nerve is positively astonishing."

"So I've been told. Will you sit?"

Spock and McCoy watched Kirk, waited to see what he would say. Kirk had no idea. His brain was frozen by conflicting emotions pushing against each other. He had no love for Conrad Franklin Kent or for anything he represented. Yet walking out could be interpreted as childish. If he stayed, Kirk felt he would win a moral victory. He said, "Gentlemen, let's sit."

Kent was pleased. He refilled their glasses, Spock's from a carafe of water. He stared into Kirk's eyes and said, "Captain, I would like you to take Hazel Payton on your voyage of investigation."

The request stunned Kirk, and for a moment he could think of nothing to say. He had not known what Kent would ask for, and this request confirmed that he was capable of anything. It was outrageous. Everybody at the table, even Kent himself, knew that it was. There was no reason for Kirk to be angry or even apologetic. He could afford to be polite. He said, "I'm sorry, but no."

"Why?"

"I don't have to justify my decisions to you, Mr. Kent. But just so that we all understand each other, let me tell you that the *Enterprise* is no pleasure cruiser, and the mission on which we embark tomorrow is no joyride. It will be dangerous, and every member of my crew will need to act at peak efficiency if any of us are to come back alive. Under these circumstances any civilian, especially a civilian whose only business is politics, will be so much excess baggage. Do I make myself clear, Mr. Kent?"

"For all the reasons you give, Captain, this mission needs to be recorded."

"We have logs, sir."

"Not good enough."

"Good enough for Starfleet."

"My point exactly."

"The answer is no, Mr. Kent." Kirk stood again and said, "Gentlemen, I believe that this time we really have overstayed our welcome. Good night, Mr. Kent."

As Kirk walked out he heard McCoy and Spock making hurried good-byes. Spock again complimented Kent's Rigellian husk. And then they were out in the corridor. Kirk was exhilarated by the drama of his exit, but he knew the feeling would wear off and he would just be angry. Angry at Kent for making an impertinent request, angry at himself for allowing the impertinent request to rile him so.

McCoy said, "I didn't think you were ever going to stop being that man's doormat."

"I'm not sure I've stopped yet. Putting Ms. Payton on the *Enterprise* is evidently important to Kent. I suspect we haven't heard the last of this."

"Indeed, Captain. We know he has the ear of many highly placed people at Starfleet Command. Surely it is only a matter of time before you hear from one of them."

Kirk strolled toward the transporter with Spock and McCoy on either side of him. Bemused, Kirk said, "There's always mutiny, of course."

Spock said, "You are already known as something of a free spirit, Captain. However, till now you have managed to avoid disobeying a direct order. Do you really wish to begin?"

McCoy said, "Don't worry, Spock. I think the captain is just indulging in a little healthy fantasy."

"I do not worry, Doctor. I am only concerned about Starfleet losing its finest commanding officer over a triviality."

"Thank you, Mr. Spock," Kirk said. "But there's no need for concern. Dr. McCoy is right. Just a little fantasy."

"What are you going to do?" McCoy asked.

"The usual, Bones. What seems like a good idea at the time."

When they returned to the *Enterprise* the only crew members awake were the night watch. Before he went to bed Kirk checked some reports and saw that the ship was ready to go. As was often the case, Mr. Scott had, with his own enthusiasm, whipped everybody into a frenzy of preparation.

The next morning Kirk was dressing when the call came in from the bridge. Admiral Nogura wanted to speak with him. Kirk grunted. He knew what Nogura wanted, but Kirk would not give it to him without a fight. "I'll take it down here," Kirk told the communications officer on duty.

A moment later the tight Oriental face of Admiral Nogura came up on the screen. He was looking down at his folded hands as if they had a message for him.

Suddenly he looked up at Kirk as if surprised to see him. "Ah, Kirk," Nogura said. He actually seemed to be embarrassed. Perhaps Nogura was not prepared to order, but only to request. If that was the case, Kirk might win this one after all.

"Good morning, sir," Kirk said.

A few seconds went by before Nogura responded. Starbase 12 was a long way out, and even a subspace radio signal took noticeable time to make a round trip.

"Is it morning there?" Nogura checked a memo-board and said, "Of course. It would have to be." He smiled at his own forgetfulness. People who did not know Nogura sometimes assumed that he was a little scatterbrained. If they tangled with him, they found out the hard way that they were wrong. "How are things, Kirk?"

"Fine, sir. We'll be underway in less than an hour."

"Good. Good. I've been speaking with Councilor Carter."

"The chair of the committee on Starfleet Operations."

"Yes." Nogura looked uncomfortable. "She sends greetings and asks a favor."

"She asks that I take Hazel Payton when the *Enterprise* goes to search for the mysterious weapon."

"Yes."

"Admiral, I've already been through this with Mr. Kent. This mission is likely to be very dangerous, and it is no place for a civilian with a camera in her head."

"Exactly what I told Ms. Carter. Will you take Payton?"

Kirk doubted if Nogura had said anything like that

77

to Ms. Carter. He said, "You can order me to take her."

"Damn it, Jim, don't force me do that. It would look bad for both of us. I'll say only that Ms. Carter and her friends can make things very hot for Starfleet."

Kirk drummed his fingers on the table but said nothing.

"Listen, Jim, I know how you feel. But the truth of the matter is that taking Payton would be good for Starfleet. Let her record anything she likes with that implant of hers, show Mr. Kent, Ms. Carter, and the rest of the Federation that Starfleet has nothing to hide."

"Take the air out of Mr. Kent's crusade."

"Exactly."

"The mission is still dangerous."

"Ms. Payton has already signed a release. She doesn't expect to be coddled." Nogura stared at Kirk. The smile was gone. Nogura thought this was serious stuff, and perhaps it was. Kirk was not happy that he could see the virtue in Nogura's argument.

Kirk said, "All right, sir."

"Very good. Spaceman's luck, Kirk."

"One more thing, Admiral, if I may."

"Yes, Kirk?"

"Have you heard anything from the Klingons lately?"

Nogura smiled and said, "You want to know how they took Kent's denial that a Federation weapon was causing their ships to disappear."

"Then you have heard from them."

"Indeed we have. And as you might expect, they

took Mr. Kent's little joke very badly. Before they stopped shouting we were forced to show them proof that Federation ships were disappearing as well. Then they wanted your exploratory mission to be a joint venture."

Kirk stiffened. The idea of a Klingon, even a Klingon scientist, walking around freely on his ship was repulsive. Kirk asked, "What was finally decided?"

"We talked them into accepting a complete log of your mission, including all scientific data and any bright ideas any of your staff might have."

Kirk let out a breath he hadn't even been aware he was holding. He said, "A person who believes that toying with the enemy is a fun idea doesn't seem like the kind I'd want for president, let alone the kind of person I'd allow to decide who I should carry aboard my ship."

"I cannot speak for the presidency, Kirk, but as for Ms. Payton, I'm afraid you're stuck. Anything else?"

"No, sir."

"Very well. Nogura out."

Kirk called the bridge and asked the communications officer to send captain's compliments to Ms. Hazel Payton and request that she come on board at her earliest convenience. The *Enterprise* would get under way at oh-nine-hundred hours ship's time, and stragglers would be left at the dock.

Despite the fact that Kirk was not getting anything he wanted, he was relieved that the subject was closed. He no longer had to fight Kent. He could concentrate on commanding the *Enterprise* and getting the crew home alive. It was possible that Nogura was right about the recordings Payton was sure to make; but even if he was not, let her take her pictures and do with them what she would.

Kirk rode the turbolift to the bridge, where things were deceptively quiet. The air was charged with tension, as it always was just before a mission began. Everything that could be done had already been done, and now it was only a matter of Kirk giving the word, of giving the *Enterprise* the single swift kick that would send it over the cliff and into the void.

Kirk settled into the command chair and felt the reins tightening in his hands as departments reported that all was ready. On the main screen Starbase 12 was pinned to the velveteen blackness of space.

Behind him Uhura said, "Ms. Payton has just requested permission to beam aboard."

"Granted. And Professor Omen?"

"Professor Omen beamed in half an hour ago with what Mr. Kyle describes as a ton of equipment."

Spock said, "I am certain Mr. Kyle exaggerates."

It would have been polite if Omen had asked Kirk's permission to board *Enterprise*. Evidently Omen did not believe in such niceties. "Where is the professor now?"

"He's in the physics lab. Ensign Plumtree is helping him set up his equipment."

"Very good. Please advise them that we get under way in five minutes."

"Aye, Captain," said Uhura.

The turbolift hissed open, and a moment later Payton came down next to Kirk's command chair. She turned her head slowly, surveying the scene as if she really were a camera. Even in the subdued bridge lighting the sensory enhancer sparkled in her hair.

Spock was of the opinion that by having the cranial interface implanted Payton had allowed herself to be mutilated. But Kirk could see a certain logic—he smiled at the familiar word—in having instant access to information, in having the ability to record under difficult or even life-threatening circumstances. But that didn't mean he wanted Payton on his ship. Though, he allowed, having her there was preferable to having a Klingon aboard.

Sulu and Chekov glanced at Kirk, willing, he knew, to follow his lead. The fact that they wanted guidance indicated that they were no more comfortable with the woman's presence than was Kirk himself.

Kirk nodded at them reassuringly, and they went back to work. He said, "Ms. Payton, you are distracting my crew."

"I don't mean to, Captain. And if I am going to make a complete record of this voyage, I need to start from the beginning."

By her own lights she was right, of course. And by Nogura's lights as well. Kirk had accepted the situation, but now that he was face-to-face with it he found it difficult to live with. He said, "All right. Just try to stay out of the way."

"Yes, Captain."

Had Payton smiled? Was she enjoying his discomfort? The smile bothered Kirk, and perhaps bothering him had been Payton's intention. She worked for Kent, and though that did not necessarily mean she agreed with his stand on Starfleet, that was the way to bet, despite her obvious feelings about Commodore Favere. Maybe she saw him as the exception that proved the rule or some other such foolishness.

"Captain," said Sulu, "we have one minute and counting."

"Thank you, Helmsman. Are we cleared for departure, Lieutenant Uhura?"

"All clear, sir."

"Very well. Mr. Sulu, all tractor beam moorings and check lines away."

"All tractor beam moorings and check lines away, aye," said Sulu.

"Helmsman, ahead one quarter impulse."

"One quarter impulse it is, sir."

Starbase 12 and the *Enterprise* became a demonstration of simple relativity. Kirk felt nothing, but on the main viewscreen Starbase 12 slowly moved to one side, and then stars poured toward him. A few minutes later Chekov said, "We are away from Starbase 12 and free to navigate."

"Course to sector 412 laid in?"

"Aye, sir."

"How long until we arrive?"

"Six hours, twenty-three minutes at warp four."

"Thank you, Mr. Chekov. Mr. Sulu, engage warp drive. Warp four for sector 412."

"Aye, Captain."

The warp engines engaged, and Kirk felt a new harmonic vibrating in his bones in so subtle a way that if he did not concentrate, he did not notice the vibration at all. In a few minutes he would forget all about it, it would become part of his being; but for the moment the single bass note was like thunder continuously rolling through every organ in his body.

Kirk stood and said, "Mr. Spock, will you accompany me to the physics lab?"

"Aye, Captain," Spock said. He pushed a few buttons on his library control board, stood, and followed Kirk to the turbolift.

With some annoyance Kirk noticed Payton coming after them. "Going to make a complete record of Mr. Spock and me greeting Professor Omen?"

"Yes, sir."

The answer was entirely without guile, but Kirk still found it easy to dislike Payton's attitude. "Very well," he said, sighing. If Ms. Payton continued to be preoccupied with such inconsequentials, she might not serve Admiral Nogura's purpose, but she also might be too busy to bother Kirk and his people while they did their work. Let Conrad Franklin Kent make a report out of formal greetings and rec room gossip.

Chapter Six

THE SILENCE in the turbolift was nervous. Kirk would
have enjoyed asking Spock if he was excited about
meeting Professor Omen at last—the gentle tweaking
of Spock was usually entertaining, a sport that both he
and McCoy enjoyed—but with Payton along for the
ride such tweaking was ill-advised. It would probably
be interpreted as a sign that Starfleet mistreated its
crew members.

Spock looked at Kirk speculatively, eyebrow up.
Kirk strongly suspected that Spock enjoyed verbally
fencing with him and McCoy and was just as disappointed by Kirk's silence as Kirk was. After all, the
space between stars was enormous, and even at warp
speeds a starship could travel for weeks or even
months without encountering anything more interesting than a hydrogen atom. Recreation was where one

found it. Sharpening one's wit was a welcome diversion, even from reading, three-dimensional chess, or a workout in the gym.

The ride was a short one because the science labs were on the deck immediately below the bridge. In the time it took to travel to Deck 2 Kirk thought of a way to give Payton back some of her own. At the closed physics lab door Kirk stopped them and said, "Ms. Payton, as far as I'm concerned, you can take a picture of anything on the ship, but Professor Omen is a civilian consultant, not a member of Starfleet. I suggest you ask his permission before you record anything." If Omen was as secretive as he seemed to be, Kirk suspected that Payton would never get that permission.

Payton nodded.

Inside they stood at the door looking across the wide expanse of the lab. One wall was a large window that could be adjusted to transmit or block any ray or particle known to Federation science. Normally it filtered out the dangerous stuff. The room was filled with big machines, dinosaurlike viewers, counters, sorters, and analyzers that dwarfed the men who worked on one of them at the far end of the room. One wore the blue shirt of the science section, and the other a simple gray coverall.

Spock asked, "Are you getting all this, Ms. Payton?"

Kirk knew he would deny it, but he suspected Spock was being sarcastic. In any case, Spock's question succeeded in surprising Payton. She said, "Why, yes, thank you."

The two man did not look up as Kirk, Spock, and Payton approached them. Kirk had met Plumtree once or twice. He was a thin man with sandy hair that seemed more like a brown cloud resting around his head than real hair. He was entirely human, but he constantly wore the expression of a worried turtle.

For a few seconds they watched Omen and Plumtree hold a machine by two handles and point the flashing probe among the circuits inside a tall metal column that supported a large cone circled with radiation rings. The metal column was as big around as an elephant's leg. The probe rang like a tiny bell as it flashed.

"May I be of assistance?" Spock asked.

The older of the two men, the one in the coverall, looked at the three of them, apparently noticing Kirk, Spock, and Payton for the first time. He was a little taller than medium height, with a muscular build and the face of a determined Pan. Beards were not popular in the Federation at that moment, but this man wore one. It framed his face in black, making him look sinister. Even his pleasant smile could not entirely dispel Kirk's impression that this man—certainly Professor Omen—generally found a way to get what he wanted and didn't worry about his methods. Kirk wondered idly who would win a test of wills between Omen and Payton.

"No, thank you. We'll manage." It was the same cultured voice that Kirk had heard speaking with Bahia Slocum. Omen sounded a little tired, as if speaking to mere mortals was difficult and not worth the energy used. He and Plumtree pulled out their probes, and Omen pushed a button that lowered the cover plate.

Kirk officially welcomed Omen and then introduced himself and Mr. Spock. When he introduced Payton she shook Omen's hand and said, "How do you do, Professor? I will be using my cranial interface to record the search for whatever is destroying our ships. I hope that you will allow me to feature your part." She waited, watching him carefully.

Omen merely glared at her. He had the blackest eyes that Kirk had ever seen. He seemed to look through her face into her mind, into her soul, into that place that held the thing that made her what she was. Payton was a beautiful woman, yes, but Omen didn't seem to be entranced by her beauty. He studied her the way he might study a natural phenomenon he was seeing for the first time. It was a powerful stare, and Payton had to look away.

Kirk expected him to refuse Payton in no uncertain terms, but instead Omen said, "Of course, my dear. Posterity must be served."

"Thank you."

"Well, Professor," Kirk said, "do you have any idea what we might be up against?"

"Theorizing in the absence of data is always fruitless, Captain. I have suspicions. Nothing more."

"Mr. Spock has a similar attitude toward theorizing. I'm sure the two of you will get along."

Now Omen's gaze raked over Spock. Spock withstood it—the immovable object to the irresistible force of Omen's stare. Omen said, "You are a Vulcan, are you not, Mr. Spock?"

"I am."

"Vulcans are known for their pacific ways. I am always surprised seeing one serving on a warship."

"The *Enterprise* is not a warship, sir. Our mission is

peaceful. We explore the galaxy, help beings whenever we can, bring Federation civilization to those who want it and would benefit by having it."

Omen said, "You forget that I designed the weapons aboard your ship, Mr. Spock. I know a warship when I see one."

"Your attitude is most unusual."

"So you say."

Omen obviously did not agree with Spock, yet he seemed unwilling to argue, maybe for the same reason he sounded so weary. Maybe he was just bored by anything he couldn't reduce to an equation. But neither Omen's boredom nor his intelligence explained the attitude Spock described as "most unusual." Kirk only wished it were unusual; it seemed very much like Conrad Franklin Kent's attitude. Starfleet was apparently surrounded by enemies where it might reasonably expect to find friends.

Hoping to change the subject, Kirk said, "Conrad Franklin Kent led us to believe that your information about the disappearances was more than suspicion."

A smile appeared briefly on Professor Omen's lips. He said, "I know only that the weapon used does not belong to the Federation."

"I see. Mr. Kent agrees with you on that, anyway. He assured me that you had some theories."

"Mr. Kent and I briefly discussed the matter of the disappearances. Perhaps he drew conclusions that I failed to see."

Kirk considered Omen's supposition to be unlikely. Had Kent lied, or had he merely been mistaken? Was Omen lying to Kirk now? Impossible to know, under the circumstances. Kirk knew only that he didn't like being lied to, no matter who the liar was or what the reason. And he found Omen's ignorance suspicious.

Short of dragging Omen down to security for a lie-detector test, Kirk had few options, and even fewer that appealed. He could bicker with Omen, send an angry message to Kent, or merely allow the situation to unfold. He was not by nature a patient man, and yet Kirk knew a hopeless state of affairs when he saw one. He could hope to learn more only by keeping his eyes and ears open. He said, "Perhaps. Congratulations on your new shield generator."

With surprising distaste Omen said, "Thank you, Captain."

Spock said, "I am curious to know how you achieved a protective field of that density and strength. The reports are vague on that subject, but I assume you have learned how to alternate the polarity of the screening fields."

For the first time Omen seemed excited. Of course, they were discussing a technical problem. "No, Mr. Spock. I have actually done something much more elegant. Instead of alternating the field as was once the custom with electric current, I actually switch the field on and off thousands of times every nanosecond."

"I see," said Spock. "That would allow the generator to establish a stronger deflector field without burning out the coils. You must have modified the delta hyperdyne."

"Exactly, Mr. Spock. Look here." He walked to a computer terminal and began to type furiously. "As you can see, the third integral becomes indeterminate when the subfrequency is high enough."

Spock nodded. "Absolutely brilliant."

"Gentlemen," Kirk said, "I'd like to stay and watch you tiptoe through the mathematics, but I have a ship to run. We reach sector 412 in something less than six hours. Will you be ready to cast your sensor net by then, Professor?"

"If you can spare Mr. Spock."

Kirk counted it a triumph that Professor Omen had thawed enough to accept Spock as a worthy coworker. "I think we can get along without him for a few hours. Ms. Payton, what's your pleasure?"

"I'd like to stay and observe for a while."

"Very well."

While Kirk rode back to the bridge alone he thought about the nest of mysteries in which he was sitting. There was the main mystery of the disappearances, of course. After that the minor mysteries crowded around, each demanding an answer. Who was lying about what, and why? Why had Professor Omen, a man who disliked publicity so much he would not show up at a dinner thrown in his own honor, allow Payton to record his activities? And why had Omen almost spit when Kirk complimented him on the successful test of his new shields?

A few hours later Spock and Omen came up to the bridge talking to each other in language so technical, Kirk did not understand one word in three, and the words he *did* understand dredged up concepts he remembered only vaguely from Academy science classes. Payton followed at a respectful distance, and she missed nothing. At the library computer console Spock and Omen began adjusting the sensors to take advantage of the machinery down in the physics lab.

Chekov said, "Entering sector 412 in ten minutes, Captain."

"Very good. Mr. Spock, are you and the professor ready?"

"Aye, Captain."

"Sulu, when we enter the sector, drop to full impulse power."

"Aye, sir."

"Mr. Spock, you and the professor may proceed at will."

"Aye, Captain."

On the main viewscreen was the star-filled void. Kirk knew that the senses of the *Enterprise* would soon stretch through the emptiness to their limits, feeling, seeing, hearing in many registers, in many frequencies, at many levels of being. If anything was out there, Spock and Omen would find it; Kirk was confident of that. He was less confident that the *Enterprise* would be able to handle whatever it was. Starships that disappeared without a trace had obviously encountered something very powerful and unusual indeed.

For a while everyone on the bridge was vigilant, watching and listening like sailors hoping for landfall. But the tension and expectation relaxed with time. Chekov sang out as each sector was covered and abandoned; people became bored with the repetition.

Payton left the bridge—to find more exciting subjects for her implant, Kirk supposed. The search continued.

"Engineering to Captain Kirk."

"Kirk here, Scotty. What is it?"

"It's that woman, sir. She won't leave my people

alone. If I didn't know better, I'd say she was also upsetting the engines."

Kirk smiled. "Is she actually preventing anyone from working?"

"No, sir, but she's making everyone nervous. We're engineers, not performers."

"Steady as you go, Scotty. Ignore her if you can."

"Aye, Captain," Scott said uncertainly.

The search went on all that day, leaving Kirk with very little to do. Every so often the tedium was broken by a call to the bridge from some section leader who would complain that Payton was poking around— asking questions, recording whatever the crew members were doing. Every time, Kirk told them approximately the same thing he'd told Scotty. He hated putting his crew through this, but Nogura had suggested it was for the ultimate good of Starfleet; an admiral's suggestion had to be taken seriously.

The watch changed, and the night crew came on duty. Spock set the sensors on automatic. If they detected anything they could not identify, he and Omen would be called immediately.

Kirk went down to the officers' mess with the rest of the day watch. He found McCoy there sullenly sipping coffee. Kirk got the meat loaf dinner and coffee from the replicator and sat down opposite him. He said, "What's the matter, Bones, lose a tongue depressor?"

"I just gave Ms. Payton and her implant a tour of sickbay."

Kirk put the best light he could on it. "Not entirely unpleasant, Bones. Ms. Payton is a very pretty woman."

"She's damned impertinent. She questioned everything—my methods, my equipment, my staff. According to her, everything we have either costs too much, is outdated, or has not been properly tested. According to her, the most modern medical facility in Starfleet is a chamber of horrors. I finally ran her off."

"I see."

"Now she's over there with that bearded man, thick as thieves. I didn't know beards were regulation."

Kirk looked in the direction McCoy had nodded and said, "That, my good doctor, is Professor Omen." Omen and Payton were whispering to each other with some urgency.

"Spock must be in hog heaven."

"It's difficult to tell."

"Yeah." McCoy drank more coffee and went on. "What do you think they're talking about?"

Kirk had been wondering the same thing. It was possible that Payton was merely interviewing Omen, but the conversation had the wrong rhythm for that; an interview usually consisted of short questions and long answers. Payton looked around as she and Omen spoke in short, hurried bursts. Not even as captain of the ship did Kirk feel authorized to demand to know the contents of a private conversation.

"Probably plotting the violent overthrow of the Federation," McCoy said.

"Probably not. Listen, Bones, I don't like having them around either. But Payton is a guest of Starfleet, and Omen is the most respected weapons expert in the Federation. They're authorized to be here, and each of them has a function." He thought of Payton and Kent putting their little documentary together. "I suppose."

"I don't know about Omen, but evidently Ms. Payton's function is to drive us all crazy."

"You exaggerate."

"Give her a few days and see if I exaggerate."

Kirk went to bed half expecting to be summoned to the bridge at any time. He lay in his bunk with his eyes open. But nothing happened, and after a while he used a Vulcan technique Spock had taught him and was able to fall asleep.

When Kirk arrived on the bridge the next morning he found Spock and Omen already at work making minute adjustments to the pattern and sensitivity of the sensor net. Payton was there, too, catching everything with her implant.

He'd barely sat down when Spock said, "Captain, we have something."

Every muscle in Kirk's body tightened. "On screen."

The view changed, and the screen showed what looked like a rock approaching them slowly. Kirk studied it for a moment before he asked, "What is it, Spock?"

Blue light shone up into Spock's face as he peered into the sensor readout. "It is an asteroid approximately five kilometers across. It is composed mainly of iron, nickel, and traces of lead. Sensors also indicate that it is fitted with a good deal of manufactured equipment."

"What sort of equipment?"

"Unknown, Captain. The readings are inconclusive."

"Magnification five," Kirk said.

The picture rippled, and the rock became an asteroid covered with sensor dishes, warp cylinders, weapons bays, and spikes, plates, and bumps that Kirk could not identify. "I don't recognize most of that gear," Kirk said, "but it doesn't look alien."

"Indeed not, Captain. Definitely of human design."

Kirk asked, "Could this be what we're looking for, Professor Omen?"

"I think I can guarantee it, Captain."

Kirk turned around. Omen was standing next to Spock watching the asteroid approach with a placid, nearly beatific expression on his face.

"Guarantee it, Professor? What do you mean by that?"

"I built everything you see there, Captain. That asteroid is my home."

Chapter Seven

KIRK WAS SO ASTONISHED that for some seconds he did not know what to say. As he surreptitiously touched the button on the arm of his chair that would bring a security team to the bridge, he asked, "Your home?"

"Yes, Captain." Omen spoke calmly. "I call it *Erehwon.*"

Spock said, "After the ideal commonwealth in Samuel Butler's book of the same name, I assume."

"Very good, Mr. Spock. I see that you are a well-rounded Vulcan."

Kirk suddenly remembered Khan and his preoccupation with John Milton. Why did the crazy ones always have an interest in the classics? Maybe large egos needed to identify with large work—it allowed them to feel superior. Maybe they felt it added credibility to their causes.

Payton watched all this with wide worried eyes, but she did not seem surprised by what Omen had said.

Spock said, "The asteroid has stopped relative to us and one thousand kilometers off our bow."

Omen continued to stand casually next to Mr. Spock, who was watching as if Omen were part of a play, with interest and yet with detachment.

Kirk stood and turned to confront Omen. "You said you knew nothing about the disappearances."

"No, Captain. I said the weapon used does not belong to the Federation, as indeed it does not. It belongs to me."

Two security men swarmed onto the bridge, and Kirk said, "Escort Professor Omen to the brig."

The lead security man nodded. He and the other man approached Omen, phasers drawn.

"The military mind is ridiculous," Omen said.

With a single deft squeeze of Omen's shoulder Spock dropped him to the deck.

"Thank you, Mr. Spock. Security, take him to the brig."

The security men lifted Omen between them and carried him away. Meanwhile Spock looked into his sensor viewer.

"Ridiculous is as ridiculous does, eh, Spock?"

"As you say, Captain."

"Anything new from *Erehwon?*"

"Erehwon is showing minimal power readings of a nature I cannot identify."

"Are we in any danger?"

"Unknown, Captain, but the amount of power in use is very small. I suggest it is maintaining status."

"Understood. Is anybody over there?"

"I see trees and what may be other decorative plants, but no intelligent life."

"Very well. Mr. Sulu, you have the bridge. Uhura, please ask Dr. McCoy to join Mr. Spock and me in the brig. And tell him to bring a medikit."

"Aye, sir."

Payton followed Kirk and Spock to the turbolift. Kirk was going to forbid her to come with them but then decided against it. She would only argue with him, and besides, he had a few questions for her.

In the turbolift Kirk asked Payton, "How much do you know about this?"

The surprise that Kirk had missed in Payton's face before came up now. She said, "Why do you ask?" Kirk was aware that everything any of them said or did was being recorded. He wondered if Payton remembered—she looked pretty shaken up.

"For one thing, Omen allowed you to record him. For another, you seemed to be expecting that asteroid or something like it."

"Ask Professor Omen your questions."

"That's what Mr. Kent always said."

"I'm saying it, too. Omen will explain everything." Kirk looked at her dubiously.

"Really," said Payton.

Kirk felt that they were reaching some sort of climax, and that Payton might be right. He would get answers at last, if not from Omen, then certainly when they explored *Erehwon.* With the arrival of the asteroid the game was certainly up; keeping secrets would be pointless. Kirk wondered if by this time tomorrow they would be on their way back to Starbase 23 and shore leave. He said, "What do you think, Spock?"

"Nothing yet, Captain. Except to observe that Professor Omen obviously has his own agenda, and the technical knowledge to carry it out."

"So far."

"Yes, sir. But I must point out that we have no idea what Professor Omen's asteroid is capable of doing."

"Care to comment, Ms. Payton?"

Payton hugged herself and leaned into the wall of the turbolift. She might know what was going on, but Kirk judged that she did not agree with it entirely. Though she was still recording, at the moment she was apparently recording the floor of the turbolift.

McCoy was waiting for them down in the brig. He glanced at Payton with distaste and said, "What's going on, Jim?"

"It seems that Professor Omen is responsible for the disappearance of the starships."

"You don't say," McCoy said. The revelation seemed to please him. He said, "I hope that Kent is in on it, too." He looked in through the security field at Omen, who was sprawled on the sleeping shelf in the cell.

"Any comment yet, Ms. Payton?" Kirk asked.

She shook her head.

"Bones, would you awaken Professor Omen?"

"What's wrong with him?"

Spock said, "I found it necessary to render him unconscious."

"The famous Vulcan nerve pinch. I see." He nodded to the security man at the doorway, and the field disappeared with a snap. McCoy entered the cell and touched Omen's neck with a hypo. It hissed, and a moment later Omen sat up groggily. McCoy stood near him, watching. Kirk knew that as far as McCoy was concerned, a patient was a patient; he didn't play favorites. McCoy waved the rest of them in, and the guard raised the field again.

"How do you feel?" Kirk asked Omen.

"I maintain, Captain. I maintain. How was it done?"

"Knocking you out? Ask Mr. Spock."

Spock said, "It was merely a matter of applied humanoid physiology."

Omen smiled weakly. "Ah, the Vulcan nerve pinch. I have heard of it but never expected to experience it. Very interesting." He mused for a moment. Kirk became impatient with the tea-party atmosphere the interrogation was taking on. He said, "We want some answers, Professor."

"Yes. Yes, of course. I am prepared to give you all the answers you are capable of understanding."

"Thanks," said Kirk dryly. He'd had a bellyful of smugly superior passengers.

"But perhaps," Omen said, "Ms. Payton would care to begin."

Payton looked startled and sat down on the shelf at Omen's feet. Omen went on, "Oh, yes, Ms. Payton. You are not just along for the ride. As Conrad Franklin Kent's chief aide you have a certain responsibility to uphold the cause."

"Cause, Ms. Payton?" Kirk asked.

Payton shuddered as she drew herself together. She said, "As you certainly know, Captain, Mr. Kent feels that Starfleet has more interest in starting wars than in preventing them."

"I've heard his theories, Ms. Payton."

"He thinks they'll help him become president of the Federation Council," McCoy said.

Payton said, "He's a politician. He can't help having a plan for becoming president any more than the captain can help having a plan of battle. Floundering around would be idiotic."

"All right," Kirk said. "I think we're getting off the track. What do Mr. Kent's theories have to do with that asteroid out there?" He hooked a thumb at the bulkhead.

Payton waited for Omen to say something. When he did not, she went on. "Mr. Kent made no secret of his feelings. Professor Omen came to him and offered to give him proof that he was right."

"What sort of proof?"

"I don't know. I don't think Mr. Kent knows either."

Kirk said, "Then as far as Conrad Franklin Kent was concerned, our mission was never to find the source of the new weapon, but to contact Omen's asteroid."

Payton shook her head. "Not exactly. I didn't know about Omen's asteroid, and I don't believe that Mr. Kent did either. Professor Omen said he had proof, and Mr. Kent sent me to record it. That's *all* I know."

"Funny priorities you people have," McCoy said.

"I didn't intend to attempt to keep *Enterprise* from searching for the weapon. As far as Mr. Kent and I knew, Professor Omen had no such intentions either."

Despite Payton's convincing arguments, Kirk felt disgust growing. When too many people had their own secret agendas, someone was bound to wind up with the short stick. Kirk disliked the suspicion that in this case he was the one. He asked, "Who else knew our real mission? Favere? Nogura?"

Payton fidgeted and said she didn't know. "Professor Omen and Mr. Kent had been communicating for a long time. My guess is that when they heard about the disappearances Professor Omen and Mr. Kent used them as an excuse to get us all together out here."

"Out here for what?"

"Out here to be part of Professor Omen's proof."

"Which you still don't know," McCoy said.

Kirk wondered if anything Payton said was true. At this point, perhaps it didn't matter. Who knew what when did not concern Kirk as much as what he would do about the situation as it stood.

After allowing a moment of silence to pass Spock said, "It seems, Professor, that it is your turn to speak at last."

Omen rubbed his forehead, and McCoy set a hand on his shoulder. Omen said, "That's all right, Doctor. My head is quite clear."

"Go on," said Kirk.

"Patience, Captain. I will tell you in my own way, and in my own good time." He rubbed the spot where Spock had pinched him. "Very interesting," he said again. "I intend to demonstrate the proof of Mr. Kent's thesis by remedying a long-standing error in my judgment."

"And that is?" Kirk asked.

"As you know, Captain, I've spent the major part of my adult life supplying the Federation with weapons of great destruction."

Kirk was inclined to argue that those weapons had been used for defense, but he didn't want to sidetrack the conversation again. "And the error in judgment?"

"Designing those weapons of war, of course. I have remedied my error by designing a weapon of peace." He half closed his eyes, then leaned over to ask Payton if she was all right. She said she was fine and waved him away.

Kirk refused to rise to Omen's bait, and apparently Spock felt the same way. Kirk was certain that before many minutes passed Omen would no longer be able to endure keeping the explanation to himself, and it would burst out of him. His ego would demand it.

McCoy said, "Are you going to tell us what a weapon of peace is, or do we have to guess?"

Good old Bones.

Omen was only partly successful suppressing a smile, and he said, "In a manner of speaking, I have built a better mousetrap. I have invented an Aleph."

They waited again. This time McCoy merely folded his arms.

Spock said, "Cantor used the aleph, the first letter of the Hebrew alphabet, to notate the transfinite number, any part of which is as large as the whole."

"Quite correct, Mr. Spock. It is also an ancient cabalistic symbol for the godhead. It is also said to be the shape of a man pointing to both Heaven and Earth, in order to show that the lower world reflects the higher."

"If you are trying to be obtuse on purpose," Kirk said, "you are succeeding."

Omen did not look at Kirk but said with annoyance, "I am speaking of difficult abstract things. I hoped that by grounding them in the culture of Earth they would be easier to understand. Perhaps I should not have tried."

"Perhaps you should get to the point," McCoy said.

"Very well, my impatient friend, I will. My Aleph is named after a literary construct in a story by a twentieth-century writer named Borges. He described his Aleph as a single mathematical point, a nexus where all parts of the universe touch, and perhaps all parts of all universes touch."

Kirk was entirely at a loss, but Spock said, "Fascinating. I have read about such things, but only as theoretical demonstrations designed as entertainment. The reality would be"—he stared at Omen—"a topological nightmare."

"Only for those who do not understand it," Omen said.

Kirk was always in awe of people who read mathematical journals for recreation. He could pilot a starship without a computer if he had to, but his mathematics was a tool that he used to solve particular problems, just as a screwdriver was meant to tighten or loosen screws. For Kirk, abstract mathematics was just so much smoke, mirrors, and tapdancing. "Nightmare or dream," Kirk said, "I don't see how a mathematical abstraction can be used as a weapon."

"The mouse rarely understands the trap, Captain. Would you be less confused if I told you that I sent every missing starship—Klingon, Romulan, and Federation—through an Aleph?"

Kirk's level of confusion was not something he

cared to discuss with Omen. He asked, "Where are they now?"

Spock was about to say something. Perhaps he knew from his reading where starships sent through an Aleph would go. In any case, he did not say but allowed Omen to answer.

Omen said, "Gone."

"Just gone?" McCoy asked. "That's a little vague, isn't it?"

"It is my best answer, Doctor. I'm not really certain myself where they go. The mathematics remains inconclusive. But I know this: I killed no one. The ships just go where they will no longer bother anyone."

"And the crews?" Kirk asked.

Omen sagged, and when he spoke he sounded tired. He said, "They are not my concern. In sacrificing their hundreds of lives I am saving thousands, millions."

"Still," Spock said, "the crews did not have a choice."

"No more than did the beings who were fired upon by Federation starships."

Kirk thought he saw a pattern forming, but parts of it were still missing. He asked, "How much did Kent know about this Aleph of yours?"

"Nothing. I promised him proof that Starfleet was warlike. That was all."

Everyone was silent for a moment.

"But there is no proof," Spock finally said.

"No proof," Omen agreed. "Only my new method for ridding the galaxy of war."

Kirk tried to be reasonable when he said, "I can understand your desire to stop war. Believe it or not,

Professor, we all want to stop war. But don't you think your method is a little extreme?"

"War and peace are extremes. Why should my method be any less so?"

Omen was obviously crazy. Still brilliant, but something had pushed him over a psychological edge. He was already in the brig, which Kirk considered to be a good first step toward preventing him from carrying out whatever his plan was. If they could get him back to Starbase 12, he would get the care he needed. Very few mental illnesses were untreatable.

Spock said, "So far, sir, you have acted in secret. It is obvious from Ms. Payton's presence that you have decided to publicize your activities."

"Correct, Mr. Spock. And that is why I so carefully used Mr. Kent to maneuver the *Enterprise* into its present position."

Omen's admission triggered something in Kirk. Suddenly he knew why Omen had gone to all the trouble. He said, "The *Enterprise* is the flagship of the fleet. It is the most desirable mouse of all."

"I hope the truth does not swell your head, Captain."

McCoy said, "I hope, Ms. Payton, that you realize you and Mr. Kent have gotten us into one fine mess."

"Mr. Kent is very sincere about his position."

"What about you, Ms. Payton?" Kirk asked.

"I am only a camera, Captain. You and Professor Omen would be doing pretty much what you're doing now even if I were not here."

"But," said McCoy, "it wouldn't become part of Kent's political campaign."

Payton met McCoy's gaze and held it. They were both certain they were correct, and in the universe of discourse, perhaps there was room for both points of view.

Payton had a reputation as a woman who got the job done. At Kent's bidding she had begun the process that had led the *Enterprise* into the dangerous position in which the ship now found herself. Payton claimed that she hadn't known what Omen had in mind, and that in fact, Kent hadn't either. Did that make her less guilty? Kirk didn't know. But he was so astonished by this whole business that he momentarily felt justified blaming anybody for anything.

On the other hand, what was Payton to Kirk or Kirk to her? She owed her loyalty to Kent, just as the crew of the *Enterprise* owed its loyalty to Kirk. But wouldn't that change if Kirk went crazy? Wasn't it the responsibility of a crew to stop taking orders, to stop being loyal, if the orders of the person in charge stopped making sense?

Apparently Kent's orders still made sense to Payton. Or they had until this conversation. Payton had never declared her own opinion of Starfleet, and that caused Kirk to suspect that she was less sympathetic to Kent's crusade than she pretended. However, even if Payton was more or less on Kirk's side, he balked at the idea of depending on her goodwill to save his ship.

And given her feelings, Kirk wondered why she worked for Kent. Many answers were possible, and though Kirk was curious, ultimately the answer didn't matter. Not now, anyway. Not at the moment. He said, "Kent was right about one thing, anyway. You, Professor Omen, were able to explain everything."

Omen nodded formally.

"Mr. Spock, have Scotty take the *Erehwon* in tow. We leave for Starbase 12 immediately. Best speed."

"Aye, Captain."

Omen stopped Spock from moving toward the corridor by saying, "Despite our discussion, Captain, you continue to underestimate me. *I* will give the orders now."

"Oh, really? And what are your orders?" He knew that Omen was powerless, yet his cold certainty disturbed Kirk.

"You will wait here until I am ready to deal with you." Before any of them could move to stop him Omen pulled back the sleeve of his uniform to reveal what appeared to be a heavily jeweled bracelet. He touched a green gem, and a cloud of transporter sparkle enveloped him. Seconds later he was gone.

"I thought the brig was insulated against transporter beams."

Kirk knew McCoy was correct. He asked, "Spock?"

"Omen's transporter effect appears to be quite different from standard Federation issue. Obviously the differences are more than cosmetic."

The ship shook once, convulsively. Kirk strode to an intercom, pounded the button with his fist, and said, "Bridge, this is the captain. What's going on up there?"

"Sulu here, sir. We're being held by some kind of tractor beam."

"Come on, Spock."

"What about her?" McCoy asked.

Kirk looked back at Payton. She seemed to be uncertain of her status, and the truth was that Kirk also had his questions. He went with his gut feelings and said, "For better or worse, she's still a guest of Starfleet." He and Spock ran for the turbolift. McCoy was not far behind. The three of them rode to the bridge, where Kirk called, "Status, Mr. Sulu?" as they walked to their stations. McCoy stood next to Kirk's chair. They all studied the asteroid on the main screen.

"No change, Captain," said Sulu. "We're being held."

"Spock?"

"Confirmed that the source of the beam is Omen's asteroid." He turned the readout selection wheel on the side of the hood and went on. "It is several orders of magnitude stronger than any known Federation tractor beam, and the energy signature is a type with which I am unfamiliar."

"Our fish seems to have caught us," McCoy said.

"All the worse for the fish. Chekov, plot a course back to Starbase 12."

Chekov pressed a few buttons and said, "Done, Captain."

"All right." He looked at Mr. Spock, who rewarded him with raised eyebrows.

"I hope you know what you're doing, Jim," McCoy said.

Kirk gave a tiny shrug for McCoy's eyes only and said, "Mr. Sulu, ahead one quarter impulse."

The ship vibrated, first at a level that was nearly

imperceptible, then more strongly. The impulse engines began to labor. The picture on the screen remained the same.

"We're not moving, Captain," Sulu said.

"One half impulse."

The vibration became a definite shuddering. The impulse engines moaned like a wounded animal. Kirk held on tight as he said, "Three quarter impulse."

"Scotty to bridge. Captain, we're shaking apart down here!"

Spock said, "Our results are nil, Captain. And we will soon permanently damage the ship."

Kirk glanced in Spock's direction. Kirk knew that expression. Spock was waiting for him to make the logical decision. And why not? Kirk had no hunches this time, so he succumbed and did the logical thing. "All right, Mr. Sulu. Cut all engines."

"Aye, Captain."

The vibration and the noise went away. They were still dead in space relative to the *Erehwon,* and none the better off for their attempt to pull it. Unless Omen had found something out there to hang on to, what he was doing was impossible.

"Is he just matching his engines against ours, Spock?" Kirk asked.

"Sensors show no engine activity."

"Then how is he holding us in place?" Kirk asked.

"Omen suggested a theory in a recent publication that might account for it." Spock became lost in a theoretical haze.

"Spock?"

"Yes, Captain. I was merely deliberating on how the theory might apply."

"And your conclusion?"

"Professor Omen spoke of a hyper-anchor. In theory, he could hold us with a tractor beam and attach *Erehwon* to the very fabric of the space-time continuum."

"It is not possible," Chekov said.

"Evidently, Ensign," Spock said, "you are mistaken."

For a moment nothing happened. The bridge was filled with waiting. Then Kirk said, "Spock, can you pinpoint the source of either the tractor beam or the hyper-anchor?"

"Aye, Captain. I have the tractor beam generator on sensors."

"Give the coordinates to Chekov. Fire phasers on my command."

"I have the coordinates," Chekov said. "Ready with phasers."

"Fire."

Kirk heard the familiar warbling of the phasers as they struck out at the asteroid. The spot where they touched flared up through the spectrum and then turned black. Kirk was reminded of the deflector test back at Starbase 12.

"Hold fire. Spock?"

"We are still being held, Captain." He turned to look at Kirk and said, "Apparently Professor Omen did not wait for the official test results before equipping his asteroid with his new shields."

Kirk knew that he had little chance of destroying the tractor beam generator or the hyper-anchor—even if he could find its source—with any weapon aboard the *Enterprise*. Omen would have made sure of that. But Kirk could not give up without a fight.

Was he thereby proving all of Omen's theories about Starfleet? Kirk had to believe in himself and in his good intentions. He was fighting to free his ship and no more. Omen could make of that what he would.

"Uhura, send a message to Starbase 12 informing them of our position and our status. Tell Commodore Favere that Professor Omen's asteroid is the source of the weapon."

Surprised, Uhura said, "Aye, sir."

"Tell him we will attempt to restrain Omen from taking any further action, and that we will transmit updates as we learn more."

Bold talk, Kirk thought. Why had no other ship sent such a message? He said, "Ready photon torpedo, Mr. Chekov."

"Aye, sir."

"Captain . . ."

"I know, Spock. Fire at will, Mr. Chekov."

The photon torpedo whooshed deep in the bowels of the ship, and a deflector field appeared around *Erehwon*. The torpedo exploded as it struck the shield. When the glare faded, everything was as it had been.

"Tractor beam?"

"Still holding, sir," Chekov said.

Uhura said, "Captain, I'm transmitting, but nothing is getting through. Some sort of interference from *Erehwon*."

Kirk rubbed his chin and said, "It really is pointless, isn't it, Mr. Spock?"

"That is my best guess, Captain."

When Payton stepped down to stand next to McCoy, Kirk said, "I hope you're getting some interesting recordings, Ms. Payton."

"Captain, I don't know what you think of me, but I assure you that I am as appalled as you are."

"I doubt if that's possible, Ms. Payton. Mr. Sulu, let's try shearing off at right angles to the beam. Full impulse power."

"Aye, Captain."

Uhura said, "Captain, I'm receiving a message from the asteroid."

"Belay that order, Mr. Sulu. Put it on screen, Lieutenant."

The asteroid and starscape wavered and were replaced by the tired, sour face of Professor Omen. He said, "Are you quite finished, Captain Kirk? You are wasting time and energy for which both of us have better use."

"Free my ship."

"That is quite impossible, Captain. The *Enterprise* is destined for a more historic role than your humble return to Starbase 12."

"You can't withstand the pounding of a Constitution-class starship forever." Kirk was only guessing, and he suspected that Omen knew of Kirk's uncertainty.

Omen said, "I designed the weapons on your ship, Captain, and I guarantee that I can. With the new technology I have developed around the Aleph, I can do as many as six impossible things before breakfast."

Now the guy was quoting *Through the Looking-Glass*. More classics. Kirk wondered where it would end.

Omen said, "No Federation ship of any class has been able to escape the Aleph. The Romulans could not escape. The Klingons could not escape. And neither will you." The screen went blank.

"End of transmission, sir," Lieutenant Uhura said.

"It looks," said McCoy, "as if we are about to go where no one has gone before."

Chapter Eight

PAYTON SAID, "Mr. Kent was right about one thing at least. Federation starships cannot perform miracles."

McCoy said angrily, "Give Jim Kirk and the *Enterprise* some time, and they'll perform miracles that'll make your head spin."

"Thank you for that vote of confidence, Doctor. Meeting in the briefing room in five minutes. Lieutenant Uhura, get that historian—what's his name, Foss? —to attend. And Mr. Scott. Mr. Spock? Doctor? You come along, too, Ms. Payton. I wouldn't want you to miss anything interesting. And Uhura—get through that interference."

"Yes, sir."

A few minutes later Kirk was sitting at the head of the briefing room table. Foss was a tall, thin man who peered around him as if he needed old-fashioned glasses and had mislaid them. He kept nervously looking at Payton, remembering where he was, and then hastily scratching notes on his memoboard with a stylus.

Kirk ordered Foss to find out everything he could about Professor Omen. "I want to know what makes him tick. I want to know his strengths and weaknesses. See Mr. Spock or one of his people if you need help with any of the technical information."

"Aye, sir."

"Well, get to it, Mr. Foss."

"Aye, sir." Foss leapt from his chair and hurried from the room.

"Options, gentlemen?" Kirk said.

Scott said, "I've read all the engineering abstracts on Professor Omen's work. If half his theories are correct, and he's built weapons based on the correct half, we're just not equipped to fight him."

"Mr. Spock, can you be a little more optimistic?"

"No, Captain. I believe that Mr. Scott has described the essence of our situation. Professor Omen has intimate knowledge of our weapons and deflectors. We have no knowledge of his, except for the small amount of information we've gleaned trying to escape. I suggest we parley."

"No technical solutions, Spock?" McCoy asked with some surprise.

"Not at this time, Doctor. But the problem does merit further study."

"Doctor? Ms. Payton?"

Payton said, "I would be delighted to record one of those Starfleet miracles for posterity, Captain."

"I'll see what I can do. Disappointing Mr. Kent would give me great pleasure. Doctor?"

McCoy studied Spock for a moment and then said, "I know what you're thinking."

"Why, Doctor," Spock said, "I had no idea telepathy was among your skills."

"You're thinking that Professor Omen's idea is logical. It makes a lot of sense. Without starships there can't be any wars."

"There is a fallacy in your argument, Doctor, and in Professor Omen's also. The members of many species were killing one another with clubs long before the invention of the photon torpedo—among them, yours and mine. If starships no longer existed, beings would find some other way to deliver their weapons. The Organians tried to bring peace to the galaxy using methods considerably more sophisticated than Professor Omen's, and even they have not yet been entirely successful."

Kirk smiled. He said, "You think that he who lives by the Aleph will die the same way?"

"I think that Professor Omen has not thought his premise through completely. Such lack of rigor frequently causes one's plans to explode in one's face."

Kirk said, "So he's not perfect. Omen may be smart, but he's neither a god nor a superman. I have confidence that anything he can invent, you and Mr. Scott can figure out."

"Aye, Captain," said Scotty. "Practical experience may work in our favor."

"See that it does, Mr. Scott. Make Professor Omen's plans blow up in his face. And hurry. We don't know his timetable."

"Aye, Captain." He stood up. "Are you coming, Mr. Spock?"

"On my way, Engineer."

"Bridge to Captain Kirk," Uhura said.

Kirk held up his hand, and Scott and Spock waited at the door.

Kirk punched the intercom button and said, "Kirk here."

"Message from *Erehwon.*"

"I can't wait," McCoy said.

"Pipe it down here, Lieutenant."

"Aye, sir."

The three-way screen in the center of the table lit up to show Omen, who said, "I assume, Captain, that you are still attempting to break away from my tractor beam."

"Assume anything you like, Professor. Did you have any other announcements? We're busy."

"I only wanted to assure you again that escape is impossible. Your ship does not have the equipment."

"You'd be surprised what sort of equipment we have, Professor. If you're going to destroy us, then do it. Your gloating gives me a headache."

The infinite weariness came over Omen again. He said, "You continue to think of me as some sort of megalomaniacal villain of the popular thrillers. I am not. I do what I must neither for recreation nor for personal gain."

"At the moment, Professor, your reasons interest me less than your intentions. Let my ship go, and I will gladly listen to you wax philosophical all the way back to Starbase 12."

"I have a counterproposal for you. I invite you and

Ms. Payton to *Erehwon,* at which time I will make it clear even to you, Captain, that what I am doing is not only desirable but necessary."

Kirk wondered if by his going to *Erehwon* the situation could get any worse. Except for wanting to be understood, Omen evidently already had everything he wanted, so holding Kirk or Payton for ransom would not be necessary. On the other hand, such a visit would certainly give Spock and Scotty more time, and Kirk might learn something useful.

Kirk touched the mute switch and said, "What do you say, Ms. Payton?"

"I'm willing if you are."

Kirk nodded and spoke again to Professor Omen. "We'll beam over immediately."

"Very good. I am sending coordinates now. And for both of our sakes, Captain, please come unarmed. Omen out." The screen blanked.

Kirk said, "He has a need to explain himself."

"Yes," said Spock. "He may drop a clue that we will find helpful in overcoming him."

"I'd rather cure him than conquer him. Any ideas, Doctor?"

"I certainly can't cure him by long distance. And not by using a single hypo full of any drug I know about, either. Psychiatry has come a long way since Freud, but it's still a subject in which a certain amount of guesswork, talent, and luck are important. In any case, Omen needs therapy, and therapy is still not instantaneous."

Kirk said, "Then we'll have to arrange it so that modern psychiatry has all the time it needs to deal with the professor." Kirk saw no way to arrange this at the moment, but he'd learned to play his cards one hand at a time. Though the future was unpredictable, to this point an opportunity to survive had always presented itself.

Kirk got a communicator from stores. A communicator was not a weapon, so Omen might not be able to detect it. As Kirk climbed onto the transporter stage next to Payton he told Mr. Kyle to keep a lock on them. "You may have only seconds to beam the three of us out."

"Three of you, sir?" Kyle asked.

"Yes. Let's see if we can't get Omen back to the *Enterprise* and make it stick this time."

"Understood."

"Energize, Mr. Kyle."

Kirk felt a moment of euphoria and disorientation as the transporter room broke up and was replaced by a room so large that at first Kirk had the impression he was on the surface of a planet.

He and Payton had materialized near a circular control station in the center of the room. Above a flat, open space atop the station was a viewscreen that currently showed a three-dimensional image of the *Enterprise*, its running lights flashing languidly. Red buttresses met high above the image. Three steps down from the control station a thin forest of delicate trees with silver leaves extended to the wall of the circular room. They stood in odd-shaped plots of open soil. Small creatures sang as they flew from tree to tree.

The place made a starship seem cramped. Not to be impressed was impossible, but Kirk tried not to show it.

Omen had added a short brown cape to his conservative gray jumpsuit. He rose from a chair at the circumference of the control station and said, "Welcome to *Erehwon*. Would you care for some refreshment?"

"I didn't come here for small talk, Professor. Say your piece and have done with it."

"I see, Captain, that like all starship captains, under the uniform and the training you are a barbarian. Perhaps I made a mistake thinking that any explanation would move you."

"Perhaps you're right. If you'll call my transporter chief, Ms. Payton and I will beam back to the *Enterprise* right now and we can all get on with our business." Kirk was bluffing, of course.

Omen stared at the three-dimensional image of the *Enterprise* for a moment and then said, "Come along, Captain. I promised you an explanation, and that is what you'll get."

Without another word Omen led them into a long hallway that shot off the main chamber like the spoke of a wheel. It was an art gallery where intricate sculptures of light and wire stood on small wooden tables, and paintings of aliens hung on the walls.

"Beautiful," Payton said.

"My daughter, Barbara, did all these." Omen indicated a holograph of a blond woman. She was a charmer, grinning and holding a speckled blue flower.

Payton strolled a ways down the corridor, looking from side to side. She said, "Your daughter is very talented."

As far as Kirk could tell, Payton was correct. He was not an artist, but he knew what he liked. He would actually have bought pieces of Barbara Omen's work for his own collection of oddly matched artifacts from around the galaxy—the ultimate compliment, as far as Kirk was concerned.

He was about to make his feelings known when Omen said, *"Was* very talented, Ms. Payton, *was.* She is dead."

"Oh. I'm sorry."

"Yes, she was a lieutenant aboard the Federation scout ship *Crockett.* She was blasted into her atomic components," Omen said with growing anger, "during a starship battle with Klingons." Omen glared at him as if Kirk were personally responsible.

Kirk said, "Nobody is drafted into Starfleet. Your daughter took her chances just like the rest of us. She obviously thought the risk was worthwhile."

"Why she was murdered is not the point. She is dead."

"You can't bring her back, no matter how many starships you destroy."

"No, but I can save others like her."

Kirk shook his head. "You can't stop Klingons from attacking if they're so inclined."

"In my universe, Captain, no one would be armed."

"We're not talking about the destruction of armament, are we, Professor? We're talking about the destruction of starships full of people, individuals as innocent as your daughter."

"Thousands suffer so that millions may live."

"Intellectual poppycock."

"You refuse to understand." He shrugged. "Perhaps it is really of no consequence."

In fact, Kirk was convinced that he *did* understand.

Before, he'd called Omen crazy, but that was only a metaphor for Kirk's conviction that Omen was terribly wrong. Now it was clear that Omen was attempting to bring back his daughter by eliminating the weapons that had killed her—weapons very much like the ones he himself had designed. The action was futile, of course; intellectually, even Omen had to know that. But guilt, and the desire of a father to save his daughter, were strong forces and not altogether rational. McCoy had been correct: Nobody on the *Enterprise* had the time or the expertise to cure Omen.

"Yes, the understanding of one starship captain is of no consequence," Omen said.

"And the destruction of one starship?" Kirk asked.

"Granted, it is only a symbolic action. But we are speaking of the *Enterprise,* the flagship. After it is gone Ms. Payton will interview me. I will explain my reasoning so that anyone who cares to listen cannot help but understand."

"That's where Conrad Franklin Kent comes in," Kirk said.

"Precisely. A man in his position will make my ultimatum much easier to deliver."

Kirk was confused. Omen wanted the galaxy to live in peace, but he wanted to do it by destroying any starship that flew by. He could try justifying that to the parties involved, but Kirk didn't think that any of them would be particularly sympathetic. He asked, "Ultimatum?"

"Yes, Captain. Certainly you don't believe that even I would be so callous as to throw starships into the Aleph without giving their crews a chance to reform."

"Reform?"

"Have I reduced you to single-word questions, Captain?"

Kirk was peeved by Omen's amusement. He said, "Answer them if you can."

Omen sighed and said, "Through the report that Ms. Payton will write for Mr. Kent I will offer the fleets of the galaxy a choice. If they will completely disarm, I will not destroy their ships."

Certainly the Klingons and Romulans would not go for Professor Omen's plan, which meant that even if Starfleet were inclined to send ships out unprotected, it would be constrained to ignore that inclination. Kirk tried to explain this prediction to Professor Omen.

Omen said, "Then what happens next will be on their heads, not mine." Omen walked back down the gallery, stopping now and then to appreciate a work of his daughter's art.

It seemed to Kirk that they had reached an impasse, and that he would learn no more from Omen. He was also curious to know how Spock and Scotty were doing. If they had succeeded in finding a way to escape the tractor beam, Omen's crackpot arguments were moot. At the very least, Uhura might have found a way to send a message to Starbase 12.

Kirk was about to reach for his communicator when Payton called, "Professor?"

Omen turned and blinked at her as if he'd been awakened.

"I'm not staying."

"What?"

Kirk was surprised, too.

Payton said, "I've watched the crew of the *Enter-*

prise at work, and I've listened to your arguments, and I've decided that no one in Starfleet is as crazy as you are. I will not write the report—at least not with the slant you want—so you might as well let all of us go."

"You are making a grave mistake, Ms. Payton."

"I don't think so. Captain, I hope it's not too late to request permission to stay with the *Enterprise.*"

Kirk smiled and nodded. "Welcome aboard, Ms. Payton." She was not the toady he'd thought her to be. Evidently, despite her feelings for Conrad Franklin Kent, she knew her own mind and had the courage to follow it.

Omen remained halfway down the gallery, as if he suspected their ideas might be contagious. He said, "Mr. Kent cannot become president of the Council without my support."

Payton said, "We'll see. Mr. Kent's political future doesn't matter as much the continued existence of the *Enterprise* and of Starfleet."

Omen shook his head sadly. "Then I must go on without you. As must Mr. Kent. Prepare to return to your ship. You are about to receive firsthand experience of the Aleph." He walked toward the main chamber.

"Stay close to me," Kirk whispered to Payton. He pulled his communicator out and flipped it open. "Mr. Kyle."

"Ready, Captain."

"What are you doing?" Payton asked.

Kirk spoke into the communicator. "On my command, Mr. Kyle. Three to beam up."

"Aye, sir."

They caught up with Omen at the entrance to the

main chamber. Kirk grabbed him by the arm, and Omen turned, astonished. "Now, Mr. Kyle," Kirk cried.

The beaming effect began, and seconds later Kirk was back in *Enterprise*'s transporter room gripping nothing. Payton stood on the transporter plate next to him, but Omen was not there.

"What happened to Omen?" Kirk cried as he leapt from the transporter stage and took in the displays on the control lectern.

Kyle was hurriedly making adjustments. "I don't know, Captain. I had him, but the carrier beam just slipped off."

"Slipped off?"

"I don't understand it myself. He seems to be shielded in some way."

"Lucky he couldn't shield us," Kirk said.

"Yes, sir."

"Or maybe it just never occurred to him to try." The idea appealed to Kirk. It was another indication that Omen was neither perfect nor as smart as he thought. Kirk reached over the wrong side of the lectern and hit the intercom switch. "Kirk to bridge. Anything from Omen?"

"Not yet, sir. And I'm still trying to find a way through the interference."

"Keep me posted. I'll be in engineering with Spock and Mr. Scott."

"Aye, Captain."

Kirk turned to where Payton still stood on the transporter stage. "You impress me," Kirk said.

"I'm glad somebody feels that way," said Payton. "I

just feel stupid. I've lost a job and a husband in one stroke."

"A husband?"

"Yes. Before we left, Commodore Favere asked me to marry him. I told him I'd think it over." She shook her head. "He'll have to understand. A woman has to do what a woman has to do."

"I hope you won't escape the commodore that easily, Ms. Payton. Scott and Spock may have some answers for us."

"Us?"

"Absolutely. You started making a report. You might as well finish it. Mr. Kent will be interested in how we perform our miracles."

"Delighted, Captain."

They hurried to engineering, where they found Spock typing numbers into a terminal and then reading calculated values to Mr. Scott, who entered them into the deflector shield matrix.

"Report," Kirk said to Lieutenant Foss, who was watching them worriedly.

"Captain," Foss said with surprise.

"I'm waiting, Foss."

"Yes, sir. I think I've found the source of Professor Omen's aberration, if I may call it that."

"You may. What is it?"

"He had a daughter who died in action aboard a Starfleet vessel."

"I know about the daughter," Kirk said. "Anything else?"

He'd astonished Foss, but Kirk didn't feel obligated to explain how he'd known about the daughter. Foss drew himself up straight and said, "Mr. Spock thinks so. One of the popular scientific journals reported that when Professor Omen finished perfecting his phased deflectors he was going to work on something entirely new, a weapon using the small dimensions."

"Small dimensions?"

"I'm a historian, sir, so I don't pretend to understand these things myself. But Mr. Spock tells me that it's the key to the entire problem."

"Very good, Mr. Foss."

"Thank you, sir."

They watched Spock and Scotty work. Spock remained calm, but Scotty became increasingly harried as he inputted the long numbers that Spock read to him. At last Scott stopped altogether and cried, "Can you not slow down a little, Mr. Spock? I'm only human." His Scottish accent was very thick now. It always thickened when he felt pressured.

Spock said, "Your humanity is not in question, Mr. Scott. But may I remind you that we have no idea how limited our time may be?"

Scotty looked pleadingly at Kirk, and Kirk said, "What's this about small dimensions, Mr. Spock?"

Spock folded his arms and said, "N-dimensional mathematics postulates that our universe extends in many directions beyond the three of space and one of time. Only our physical and mental limitations prevent us from experiencing them. Dimensions eleven through twenty-seven are said to be the small dimensions because they do not, in fact, extend at all."

"I don't understand. How can they be dimensions if they don't extend?"

"I assure you, Captain, these conclusions emerge directly from the mathematics."

He'd heard Spock's mathematical lectures. Kirk's head sometimes rang for days afterward, and he was none the wiser. "I'm sure they do, Mr. Spock," Kirk said. "How does all this help us?"

"I am working on the assumption that Professor Omen's Aleph is the weapon he was speaking of in the journal, and that it is based on his work with N-dimensions."

"And?"

"And using what I know of N-dimensional geometry, Mr. Scott and I are readjusting the shields so they will deflect the Aleph. Rather than engulfing the ship, the Aleph's impact will knock the *Enterprise* free of the tractor beam."

"You're sure of this?" Kirk asked.

"We are confident," Spock said.

Kirk looked at Scotty, who shrugged.

"Very well, gentlemen. Get on with it. I'm going to the bridge. Ms. Payton?"

"I've seen enough here."

"Come along, then."

Kirk used the time on the turbolift to study Payton. She had surprised him more than once with her ingenuity and courage. She was, as Kent had told him, a woman who got the job done. Kirk felt his admiration warming into affection, but he knew that such feelings were pointless. If they survived the Aleph, she would be going back to Favere. If they did not, time was very short.

At the moment Payton appeared to be worried,

which was surely the rational reaction to what was going on. Kirk smiled and said to her, "We've gotten out of worse messes."

"Mr. Spock said he was only confident, not certain."

"I'd sooner bet my life on Mr. Spock's confidence than on somebody else's certainty. As a matter of fact, I have. We'll be fine."

"And if not?"

Kirk opened his hands as if releasing the thought. He said, "It will cease to matter."

"To us, anyway."

Kirk nodded. Those who were left behind sometimes suffered the most.

McCoy was already on the bridge, speaking in low tones with Uhura. When Kirk sat down in his command chair McCoy stepped down to stand at his left hand. "You can cut the tension on the ship with a knife, Jim."

"Not much longer, Bones." Kirk bit a knuckle as he studied *Erehwon* floating among the stars. He couldn't destroy the thing; he couldn't run away from it; arguing with Omen was useless. What clever maneuver was he overlooking?

"I suppose Spock and Scotty are hammering together some machinery of salvation down in engineering."

"They are, and—"

"Captain?" Uhura said. "Message from Professor Omen."

"On screen."

"It's for Ms. Payton."

"On screen will be fine, Lieutenant," Payton said.

Omen appeared looking sadder and more tired than

usual. Or maybe he was just bored. He said, "Ms. Payton, I will offer you one more chance to return to *Erehwon.*"

"And I will offer you one more chance to return with us to Starbase 12."

"I'm sorry, Ms. Payton. Captain, if you have prayers to say, I suggest you say them now."

Uhura came up to Kirk's right-hand side and whispered in his ear, "Mr. Spock reports that he and Mr. Scott are ready."

Kirk made a small nod and said, "Thank you, Professor. Any other bits of advice you have for us?"

"You're dying for a good cause, Captain."

Kirk no longer wanted to speak with Omen. He no longer wanted to look at him or even think about him. Kirk had rarely been in a situation where he felt more helpless. He said, "Opinions differ on that, Professor. Kirk out."

Omen was replaced by *Erehwon* and the stars. "Ten," Omen said.

"Spock to Captain Kirk."

"Nine," said Omen.

"What is it, Spock?"

"Eight."

"I wish to recalibrate the sensors to better record the Aleph."

"Seven."

"No time, Spock. Seven . . . six seconds and counting."

"That is unfortunate."

"Five."

Spock went on, "This is an unprecedented opportunity to confirm various theories of N-dimensional geometry."

"Four."

"Some other time, Spock. You are the best first officer in the fleet." Kirk gripped the arms of his chair. Everyone he could see—McCoy, Payton, Sulu, Chekov—braced themselves any way they could.

"Three."

"Thank you, Captain"

"Two. One. Farewell, *Enterprise*."

Chapter Nine

A TINY BRIGHT SPOT appeared on *Erehwon*. As it rushed toward *Enterprise* it grew into a spinning diamond. And then Kirk saw that the spinning was an illusion. Moving across the surface of the diamond were uncountable objects, scenes, and people. The Aleph came quickly, so Kirk did not have time to study it, but in the few seconds he had it showed him Lieutenant Foss down in his cabin, a green hill on some planet like Earth, the glare of a star's interior, colorful spider creatures crawling across bare rock in a single line that extended to the red horizon, a child with an ice cream cone, shattered and abandoned domes on Earth's moon—all this and more, all without confusion, all without overlapping, all at a single point.

And then the Aleph struck the *Enterprise* with such force that the ship leaned to one side like an ocean-going vessel hit by a tidal wave. Lights flickered, and the superstructure moaned. Suddenly the *Enterprise* snapped free from the tractor beam, causing *Erehwon* to seem to fly off one side of the main viewscreen.

Kirk cried, "Sulu, ahead full impulse, any course."

"Aye, sir. Sir, navigational sensors inoperative. Shields down."

"Get us out of here now, Mr. Sulu."

"Aye."

The impulse engines hummed as the stars crawled across the main screen. Apparently only visible light sensors still worked. That was fine. Scotty would repair the sensors and the shields. But the *Enterprise* had to get out away from *Erehwon* before any repairs could be done, and for the first time Kirk allowed himself to believe that they had actually made it.

"Is everybody all right?" Kirk asked.

They were all shaken up but uninjured.

Kirk hit the button that would put him through to engineering. "Gentlemen, you did it," he said.

"Aye," said Mr. Scott, "but my poor shields will never be the same."

Spock said, "I assure you, Captain, that returning the shields to their original state is a simple matter."

"Is there any advantage to doing that?"

"None as far as I can determine, Captain. Our protection from the Aleph did not cost us efficiency in other areas."

"Very well. Get started on repairs. Kirk out. Mr. Sulu, take us back to Starbase 12, warp six."

"Aye, sir."

Chekov said, "Incoming, Captain."

Kirk gave his attention back to the screen and saw a bright point of light approaching. As it grew into a spinning diamond Kirk's heart sank. Without shields of any sort the *Enterprise* was a sitting duck.

"Warp six now, Mr. Sulu."

The stars sprang away from them, but the Aleph stayed on their tail. The damned thing could follow the ship into warp space! Small dimensions, indeed. In warp space their ability to maneuver was limited.

"Mr. Sulu, drop to full impulse and take evasive action."

"Aye, Captain."

The stars jumped in crazy patterns, but the Aleph never wavered. As it rushed toward the *Enterprise* the surface of the diamond became the discrete bits of the infinite universe.

This time, when the Aleph struck the ship, Kirk felt no impact, as if the Aleph was a hole that had engulfed it.

The main viewscreen remained empty. And yet it wasn't blank. It was the color Kirk saw when he closed his eyes in a dark room. The color on the screen had depth and near-solidity. It was hypnotic.

The impulse engines were still running, but now they were laboring, chugging along almost like the gasoline engines of the twentieth century. Kirk yawned. He suddenly felt very tired. He'd been under a lot of stress lately, but that would not entirely explain the fatigue.

"Have we lost visible light sensors, too, Mr. Chekov?"

Chekov plodded to Spock's station and looked into the viewer. "No, sir. Main viewscreen is functioning properly."

"Then where the hell are we?"

"I don't know, sir."

Kirk punched the intercom button on his command chair and said, "Mr. Scott."

"Here, Captain."

"How long will it take you to repair the sensors and the shields?"

"I have a team working on each of them now, sir."

"How long?"

"I canna say, sir. The shield generators—well, we can have them on line in a few minutes. But most of the sensor receptors are gone, and that beastie burned out entire banks of circuits. It could be days."

"Make it hours, Scotty. Our survival may count on those sensors."

"Aye. We'll work 'round the clock. Scott out."

Kirk tried to think, but his mind seemed thick and unresponsive. He asked Uhura if she had gotten through to Starbase 12.

She said, "No."

Without a squawk, then, the *Enterprise* would seem to have vanished as mysteriously as the other missing ships. Kirk said, "Mr. Sulu, take one minute to turn the ship three-sixty degrees."

"Aye, sir."

Nothing changed on the main screen, and Kirk had to ask if the ship was moving. His body felt as if it were made of lead.

"Inertial guidance says we're turning at one rpm."

Spock arrived on the bridge, and Chekov, looking

grateful, went back to the navigator's station. The Aleph edged onto the screen.

"Range?"

"Unknown, Captain," Spock said.

The ship continued its sweep, and the Aleph crawled off the screen. Eventually Sulu said, "Inertial guidance says we're back where we started."

"Speak to me, Spock," Kirk said.

"Without sensors I would be only guessing."

"Guess then."

"We are in a universe in which only two things exist: the *Enterprise* and the Aleph that brought us here."

Kirk said, "Omen has been sending ships through the Aleph for months. Where are they?"

"Maybe out of visual range," Uhura said.

"Doubtful, Lieutenant," Spock said. "The mathematics suggest that the other side of any Aleph will be a random point inside the universe of universes."

"You mean that each ship will come out in a different universe?"

"Each ship *can* do that. There is a small probability that two ships will meet on the far side of two different Alephs. Remember, the destination is random."

So they were probably alone, without even the cold comfort that came from sharing a disaster with another ship. If they were to be saved, they would have to do it themselves. Kirk said, "Then we can't even go back through the Aleph."

"We can, Captain, but we have no assurance that we would be any better off than we are now."

"Or any worse off," said McCoy.

"Indeed, Doctor. The mathematics of the Aleph's geometry offer us little hope either way."

"What do you know about hope?"

"I know that you humans value it highly, particularly when you have nothing else."

Kirk said, "It's not logical, Mr. Spock, but we will continue to hope." He wished that he saw cause for optimism, but strain as he might, he couldn't even force his brain to work very well. Everyone on the bridge seemed to be as tired as he was. McCoy was leaning against the arm of his chair, and Payton was watching the main viewscreen while she sat on the steps to the upper level with her head resting on one fist. Kirk had complete confidence in Mr. Scott and his teams, but if they were suffering from the same numbing fatigue as everyone on the bridge—and he had no reason to believe they were not—then everything would take longer. Even Scotty's prediction of days might be overconfident.

Suddenly McCoy said, "It's like the negative energy zone around that giant amoeba we blew up."

For a moment everyone considered McCoy's statement.

Then Spock said, "Doctor, you may have accidentally said something useful." He turned to study the readouts at the bottom of his viewer.

McCoy smiled for a moment and then asked Kirk, "What did he mean by that?"

Kirk shook his head. He wondered what Spock could be looking at. The sensors had been burned out by the Aleph, and even if they had not, Spock himself had admitted that there was nothing but emptiness around them. It was possible that Spock had a hunch, and, being a Vulcan, he would never admit it. Vulcans believed in probabilities, not hunches. When the hunch became something Spock could support with facts, Kirk would hear about it.

"If Dr. McCoy is correct, where are the amoebas?" Chekov asked.

"Where indeed?" said Kirk.

"What amoebas?" Payton asked, entirely bewildered.

A few hours ago Kirk might have kidded Payton about not keeping up with Starfleet reports, but she had chosen to be there. She was one of the crew now, as much at risk as any of them, and a straight question deserved a straight answer. Kirk organized his thoughts, but only with difficulty. He said, "In sector 39J we encountered a single-celled creature that was many thousands of kilometers across. It generated a black zone much like the stuff outside." He gestured vaguely at the viewscreen. "The zone absorbed all energy generated inside it. Including metabolic energy. Bones, could that be happening to us again?"

McCoy continued to stare straight ahead.

"Bones?"

"Oh, sorry, Jim." He shook his head. "I must have been daydreaming. Yes, it certainly could be happening to us again. I hope not. I almost ran out of stimulants last time."

Kirk smiled and said, "You should have been here, Ms. Payton. We pulled off one of our famous miracles." He really needed a nap.

"I still say Spock botched the acetylcholine test."

Spock said, "I fail to see why bringing that up continues to please you."

"You're right, Spock. Childish of me." McCoy winked at Kirk.

"But you are quite correct in comparing the amoeba incident and the situation in which we find ourselves."

"What is it, Spock?" Kirk asked.

"At this time, Captain, my theory is only partially formulated. But I will say this: The doctor is likely to run out of stimulants."

"Run out," McCoy repeated. He shook his head once more and said, "I'd better get down to sickbay and see if anybody needs me." He walked to the turbolift like an old man, frowning as if he were trying to remember something. "I'll be back," he said before he left. "Y'all will need stimulants, too." The turbolift doors closed.

"Should we expect amoebas, Spock?"

"Impossible to say. Without sensors we are limited to what we can see on the main screen. Computer analysis is impossible. However, the lack of stars would indicate that the situations are comparable, whatever their origins."

Payton said, "Maybe the amoebas ate everything and then died of starvation. Over the millennia they disintegrated back into the fabric of space."

"It is possible," Spock said. "But without sensors to tell us whether the space around us is truly empty or filled with microdebris, we cannot say for certain."

"We will all die," Chekov said calmly.

"Belay that talk, mister," Kirk ordered. "As long as we're alive and thinking, we have a chance. We're not amoebas. Spock, get down to engineering and help Mr. Scott's sensor team. With sensors we might be able to learn something useful from the proper study of the Aleph. There must be a way for us to control our destination on its other side."

"You may be right, Captain," Spock said as he headed for the turbolift. Despite his Vulcan constitution, even he was slowing down. The unspoken corollary to Spock's statement was, of course, that Kirk could be wrong. After all, Kirk couldn't be the first starship captain to suggest his science officer try to get them home.

"A better mousetrap," Kirk said with disgust.

By the end of the ship's day *Enterprise* energy levels were down fifteen percent, and Kirk was certain that his own energy levels had dropped considerably more than that.

His weakness and lack of energy depressed him and made him angry. Kirk was a man who had always taken good care of himself—eating the recommended foods, working out in the gym when his schedule had allowed. Now all his hard work—it seemed—had gone for nothing, stolen from him by this universe, this infinite expanse of nothing. This universe brought him and the laziest of creatures to the same level, as death brought all creatures to the same level.

He did not normally have such thoughts. A starship captain must be an optimistic and clever person, in addition to the other attributes he or she might have. For one thing, Kirk was a philosopher king, a supreme and benevolent leader in his twenty-three-deck realm. And like any man, Kirk had his theories about the rules of life, many of them—as Spock had pointed out—more whimsical than rational. Rules came and went over the years. For instance, Kirk had not believed for a long time that pulling the bed covers over his head would save him from monsters. One of the few rules that remained a foundation of his life was that he must believe in himself above all. This universe attempted to drain that belief from him, but he fought against it even as he fought the depression and anger.

Kirk had Uhura shut off the viewscreen. This not only saved a small amount of power, but the dead screen was an improvement: It was only blank; it did not show them the unnerving darkness of the universe outside. And the Aleph was hypnotic; watching it, the bridge crew quickly became spellbound and forgot about their jobs. There wasn't much to do on the bridge at the moment, but Kirk liked to have his on-duty personnel alert even so.

They had no call to use up power running either warp or impulse engines. As Chekov had pointed out, when each point outside the ship was exactly like all the others, the concept of motion was meaningless anyway. Chekov sighed and, with a smile on his face, recalled a dark, crowded nightclub in Moscow where the concept of motion had also been meaningless, but for a different reason.

Sickbay was a mob scene, and McCoy had taken to sending all but the worst cases of fatigue back to work full of stimulants. Some crew members returned to sickbay terrified by what they had seen. Nightmare creatures climbed from access holes in the decks to menace them, only to disappear along with their holes as they were about to set fang, claw, or tentacle on the crew member. Other crew members reported seeing bulkheads run like waterfalls, or strangers looking out at them from mirrors.

As tired as he was, Kirk walked the ship, giving comfort and encouragement where he could. Down in engineering he tried to help repair the sensors until Mr. Scott suggested, in the most diplomatic way imaginable, that his talents might be better used elsewhere.

Ms. Payton followed Kirk everywhere, always recording, though if the recordings were filtered through her senses, they could not be any too clear or even coherent. Despite the stimulant McCoy had given her, her progress became more and more sluggish. The truth was, they all came to move like small children on their way to bed after a busy day. Kirk liked Payton more and more all the time, for her bravery, for the strength of her moral conviction, for the tenderness with which she treated fragile crew members.

Down on Deck 17 Kirk and Payton were horrified to discover a ragged hole blasted in the outer bulkhead of the ship's hull. They could look directly onto the blankness. A crewman was looking at it, pointing to it, laughing hysterically.

Payton rushed to him and put a hand on his shoulder. "It's all right. It's all right. The hole isn't really there. Is it, Captain?" She sounded uncertain.

Kirk could not remember having been so tired, and without making a constant effort he might have slid into hysteria himself. But at the moment he was fascinated by the hole. It could not really be there, of course, or this entire section of the ship would have been open to hard vacuum and sealed off. Carefully, slowly, he reached out a hand. And sure enough, when he touched what seemed to be open space the hole was briefly replaced by the face of a snarling Klingon, and then by blank bulkhead.

The crewman continued to laugh, and Payton hugged him. The laughter stopped, but the crewman began to shriek and cry. Kirk could see that Payton's methods were not working, and eventually he had to slap the crewman to get him to stop.

"Go to sickbay," he ordered the crewman. Solemnly the crewman stumbled off in the right direction.

Some hours later Kirk called a meeting in the Deck 7 briefing room. When he got there the table seemed to be sagging at both ends as if it were made of taffy. It reminded him of a painting done a few centuries before, with clocks draped over tree limbs. He blinked, and the table became as flat and solid as it had ever been.

Soon after, Spock, Scott, and McCoy arrived, as well as Ms. Payton, implant still in place. Kirk had entered commendations for all of them in his log. If the *Enterprise* got home safely, Payton would supply Conrad Franklin Kent with quite a document, though not the one he'd expected.

After they had gathered they sat hunched over the table, breathing with difficulty, as if they had just run a long distance.

Kirk said, "Did that hysterical crewman get to sickbay all right?"

"Which hysterical crewman?" asked McCoy. "I've seen a bunch of them this morning."

Kirk was about to describe the crewman he and Payton had helped and then decided that it didn't matter. A sick crew member could not wander the corridors of the *Enterprise* for long before somebody helped him or her to sickbay.

"Report, Mr. Scott."

Scott looked up at Kirk and said, "Power levels are down twenty-seven percent and continue to fall at a few percentage points an hour."

"Then we have time to find a solution."

"Aye, Captain. We have time, but we may not have the strength."

"Scotty's right," McCoy said. "The crew's metabolic processes are running down at about the same rate as the ship's batteries. The difference is that long before the batteries are dead we will all have fainted. I'm doing what I can for everyone, but it isn't much."

"Stimulants have only a limited usefulness."

"Right. On the drugs, we're using up the energy we have much more quickly—essentially robbing our future in order to work now. Eventually we'll all just burn out."

Kirk and the others contemplated the future that McCoy presented them with.

McCoy said, "The simple fact, Jim, is that we don't belong in this universe. But we'll die here if we don't leave soon."

"You know, Bones, I look back fondly on the simple days when all we had to do was destroy a giant spacefaring amoeba."

"Aye, Captain," said Scott. "As tired as I am, I'd throttle the beastie with my bare hands."

"I appreciate your willingness, Mr. Scott. What about the sensors and the shields?"

"Sensor components are fused into a single block. Working at our present rate, you won't have them for several hours. Shields are about ready now."

"Shields have never been so useless," McCoy said.

"Best speed, Mr. Scott. Spock, do you have anything to add to our list of disasters?"

Spock was bearing up better than any of his human crew mates, but even he drooped in his chair and leaned on the table with his elbows. He said, "I have no new disasters to report, Captain. Not as such. I will only add that the hallucinations crew members have been reporting, and which I have experienced myself, lead me to believe that this universe is causing a great strain on the fabric of reality aboard the *Enterprise.*"

Kirk said, "It's always nice to have one's suspicions confirmed. Anything else, Spock?"

"I hesitate to encourage you in any way, Captain, but I believe I have found a substitute for our sensors."

"You'll be able to study the Aleph?" Kirk asked. It had been a long time since he'd felt this much enthusiasm.

"Does that mean we can go home?" Payton said.

"I do not guarantee a solution," Spock said, "but I believe that using my method, we can significantly improve our chances of escaping from this universe."

Chapter Ten

"DON'T KEEP IT to yourself, Spock," Kirk said.

"It will involve Ms. Payton's cooperation."

"You have it, Mr. Spock. What is your method?" Payton seemed surprised that she had spoken to Mr. Spock in this way, and she blushed.

"I believe," said Spock, "that by modifying Ms. Payton's implant I will be able to use it and her as a primitive sensor."

Scotty thought about that for a moment and then said, "Aye. It might work. You'll have to use some of the equipment Professor Omen left behind."

"Indeed, Mr. Scott. I will also require your skills as a technician."

Kirk asked, "This will take less time than repairing ship's sensors?"

"I expect so, Captain. In any case, Mr. Scott's

147

engineering team will continue to repair ship's sensors while he and I jury-rig Ms. Payton's implant. We will not be competing, but I suggest that one of us will surely finish before the other."

"And we're ahead either way. Very good, Mr. Spock. Get up to the physics lab. And remember . . ." Spock, Scott, and Payton stopped at the door and looked back at him. They were tired. Everyone on the ship was tired. "Remember that we're not just attempting to save ourselves. We must get home and stop Professor Omen."

Spock and Scott left with Payton.

Kirk and McCoy continued to sit at the table breathing hard. McCoy said, "Omen's crazy, isn't he?"

"The evidence seems conclusive. What's the problem, Bones?"

"I've been a doctor all my adult life. When I was a kid I wanted to be a doctor. I never questioned whether curing the sick and comforting the wounded was a good idea. But here we are, trying as hard as we can to prevent somebody from stopping war."

"You heard Spock, Bones. Omen won't stop war. He's just destroying starships."

"Maybe destroying starships and stopping war are the same thing."

Kirk was glad that Payton wasn't there to record this conversation. How would McCoy's arguments come across to the civilians back home? Would everything he said make great propaganda for Kent? Kirk decided that he had enough to worry about without adding politics to the list. He said, "Sorry you joined Starfleet, Doctor?"

McCoy thought for a moment and then said, "No, Captain. Of course not. It's just that at the moment I'm a little tired, that's all. Stopping wars seems like a good idea."

"It is a good idea, Bones. Omen's just going about it the wrong way. You can't stop wars by killing people."

McCoy nodded for what seemed to be a long time. Then he stood up slowly and briefly supported himself on the table with his hands. He said, "If it's all right with you, Captain, I'll get back to sickbay. It's amazing, but sometimes people feel better just going to a doctor, even if the doctor can't do much for them but hold their hand and tell them exactly how bad things are."

"Not logical, is it, Bones?"

"No. But it works. Sometimes it even works on Vulcans, if they're in the mood."

Kirk said, "Go ahead," and he watched McCoy stagger from the room. He was older than most of the other crew members, and this universe was harder on him. It hurt Kirk just to watch him move, yet there was nothing Kirk could do for him.

As a matter of fact, until Spock and Scotty made their modifications there was nothing much Kirk could do for the *Enterprise*. It was unlikely that he would be needed on the bridge anytime soon. This universe was empty. By definition, nothing ever happened in it. The *Enterprise* and the Aleph were new, of course, but Kirk doubted if they would be joined by anything more of a similar magnitude.

Briefly he considered helping McCoy, but having the captain mucking around in sickbay would probably make McCoy nervous. Besides, as captain, Kirk needed to maintain an air of authority, and that would be difficult when carrying bedpans, even if they were only metaphorical.

At last Kirk went up to the physics lab. Watching Spock and Scott make progress with the implant would give him something to do and make him feel better. He could talk with Payton. That would be a comfort, too.

Spock and Scotty finished modifying the implant before the team down in engineering repaired the sensors. Scott seemed hurt by this, as if his people had, in fact, lost a competition, but he was enthusiastic about the implant. The fact that Spock also thought it would work was encouraging.

Spock went to Payton's cabin, where she kept the equipment that monitored and recorded the signal from her implant. Payton came up to the bridge and sat in Spock's chair. Her implant looked the same to Kirk, but in this case, as in many others, appearances weren't everything.

Spock's plan was for Payton's eyes to act as primary sensors. Whatever she looked at—in this case, the Aleph—would be funneled through Professor Omen's equipment, evaluated, filtered, and sent to Payton's own equipment in her cabin. There Spock would view the Aleph and attempt to analyze it. He would be helped by the limited computing power available to Payton's monitor, but because there was no way to automatically input Payton's sensory data in the ship's computer, the work would move slowly and perhaps ultimately prove to be impossible. Still, it was worth a try—it was the only chance they had.

Kirk walked over to her and asked, "How do you feel?"

She smiled tiredly and said, "How do any of us feel? Well enough to get the job done." She glanced at the empty viewscreen.

Soon Kirk would order the screen activated again. He would order his people to ignore the Aleph as best they could, make it a priority to watch their instruments, and hope for the best.

"Spock to bridge."

"Kirk here. Are you ready?"

"Yes, Captain. Ms. Payton's equipment is quite elementary."

Spock's comment amused Payton.

Kirk walked up to stand next to her. He said, "I won't let you fall into the Aleph too far."

"What about Spock?"

Spock said, "I believe that my powers of concentration are adequate for the task at hand."

"I'm sure they are," Kirk said. "Ready, Ms. Payton?"

She nodded.

"All right, everyone. Attend to your instruments. I don't want a bridge full of somnambulists."

There was polite laughter among the crew.

"Lieutenant Uhura, let's have visual."

"Visual, aye, Captain."

And suddenly there was the Aleph spinning and sparkling against the void. Even his limited experience with the Aleph told Kirk that the spinning and sparkling were illusions; he was seeing every component of the universe playing itself out at a single point. With difficulty he turned away from the Aleph and looked at Payton. Her eyes were wide; she seemed barely to be breathing.

"Ms. Payton?" Kirk said.

"It's beautiful, Captain. I see . . . everything."

She was still capable of answering him. They could continue for a while yet. He called to Spock, but there was no response.

"Spock," Kirk called, now worried.

"Here, Captain," Spock said. His body and mind were functioning properly, which pleased him. The pleasure did not have an emotional component, it simply told him that everything was going according to plan. The Aleph was fascinating but difficult to look at. So many parts of the single point demanded his attention. He recorded the Aleph and discovered that the playback gave him only its gross structure. All detail was lost. Apparently Ms. Payton's equipment was not sophisticated enough to pick up the Aleph's infinite subtleties. Perhaps no machine was sophisticated enough.

By changing the focus of his attention on the direct input he could look at anything he desired. The choice was almost overwhelming, even for someone with the disciplined mind of a Vulcan. He saw everything at a single point, with no confusion, with no overlapping, with no crowding. Each thing, each action was discrete, alone, a universe among universes, an inspiration for new philosophies.

He saw Captain Kirk pacing on the bridge; crew

members drinking coffee in the rec room; his father pondering the words of an ancient Vulcan scroll; a part of the galaxy where the stars seemed to touch and feed one another swirling incandescent gases; creatures with great teeth fighting under an alien ocean; teeming cities; a mountain range reflected in a single teardrop on a young girl's face; the molten center of a planet; a bacterium; a lizard creature using natural body acid to lick its way out of its shell; a great black space fleet. Spock could look over his own shoulder.

"Fascinating."

"What's that, Spock?" Kirk asked.

"I am attempting to correlate my data, Captain."

Spock felt himself drawn into the Aleph. If he was having trouble maintaining his separateness from the thing, certainly Ms. Payton would find it more difficult. He touched a slider. Input from the Aleph flowed into the monitor's computer as well as into his own brain. Together they dissected, analyzed, detected, deduced, calculated. The interplay occurred faster than it could be told, as fast as thought.

Spock erected geometrical models in his mind. They looked like cubes, tetrahedrons, tesseracts, and tesseracts of tesseracts, shapes that extended along dimensions where Spock's intelligence had never gone, had never conceived of going. He rotated the shapes along their small axes.

Suddenly the Aleph was gone, and, surprised, Spock nearly fell off his chair. He held on to the table tightly and used a Vulcan technique to regain his mental equilibrium. For some reason Payton had stopped looking at the Aleph. Had she fainted? Had the captain pulled her away from the viewscreen?

"Captain, I trust that everything on the bridge is all right."

"Fine, Spock. Fine." Payton had stopped answering when Kirk spoke to her, and the irises of her eyes were open wide. She didn't move. Kirk said, "Uhura, end transmission now." The screen went blank. He called for medics and then told Spock that Payton had mentally fallen into the Aleph, and he was taking her to sickbay. Seconds later two orderlies arrived and carefully loaded Payton onto an anti-grav stretcher.

Kirk followed them down to sickbay, where McCoy got Payton situated on a diagnostic couch and impatiently ran his hand scanners over her. All the while McCoy made the noncommittal grunting noises that practitioners of his trade had been making for hundreds, perhaps thousands, of years. When he was done he pulled again and again at his lower lip.

"Well?" Kirk asked.

"She's fine, Jim. Exhausted, but other than that, fine."

"Doctor?"

They turned and saw Spock, his face a peculiar greenish gray, leaning against a doorway. Kirk was startled by this. Spock liked to keep up a strong front when he was sick, as if germs and injuries affected him no more than emotions. He made allowances for the frailties and defects of others, but he claimed to have complete control over his own body, and he saw sickness as an impediment to doing his duty.

Kirk and McCoy helped him to a chair, and Spock said, "I am quite all right, Doctor. I merely came to sickbay because I was concerned about Ms. Payton."

"She's fine. You'll stay in that chair till I tell you you can get up." McCoy ran a medical tricorder over him and said, "You're a matched set with Ms. Payton, Spock. She shows all the symptoms of a kid who's been too long at the fair. Too much input. Over-excitement—"

"Doctor!" Spock said, shocked.

"Overstimulation, then. Call it what you will, you'll either rest now, or I'll strap you in bed for a week."

"Threats will not avail you, Doctor. If I rest now, we will certainly be dead in much less than a week." Despite his prediction, Spock did not attempt to stand.

"What is it, Spock?" Kirk asked.

Spock said, "Being in this universe does have certain advantages. Because the *Enterprise* and the Aleph are the only two significant objects, discovering how the Aleph works is a much simpler matter than it would be in a universe such as our own, where the other masses would only complicate my calculations."

McCoy said, "Only you could see an up side to an empty universe."

"So our chances improve," Kirk said.

"Yes, Captain. But not enough. The doctor has accurately diagnosed my physical state. Though I fight against the characteristics of this universe, I find myself progressively more tired. My mind is not functioning at anything near optimum efficiency. Processing the images presented by the Aleph adds an extraordinary load. Not even the Vulcan mind is so constructed that it may look on infinity with equanimity. Also, because of the strain on the fabric of reality, I do not entirely trust the evidence of my own eyes."

McCoy said, "At last we'll get a chance to see if the computers work."

"The situation is not that simple, Doctor. Because of the state of our sensors, I must select and input the data manually. The amount of data necessary is enormous."

"I don't understand," McCoy said angrily. "We came through that Aleph. Our universe must be on the other side."

"I remind you, Doctor, that Alephs do not work in that fashion. We have no way to know what is on the other side. The destination may be changing from instant to instant. At the moment we go through, the universe on the other side of the Aleph may be even more incompatible than the one in which we find ourselves. The physical laws of that universe may cause us to dissipate, or even to explode instantly, or they may cause us to suffer long, painful deaths. The mathematics are not helpful on this point."

Spock allowed them to absorb these facts. Kirk knew that a good part of the hopelessness he felt was caused by the nature of the universe they were in; yet the picture Spock painted was not a pretty one.

Spock continued his lecture. "My preliminary work has shown me a still more unusual fact: Even if our universe is on the other side of that Aleph, our presence in this empty universe, a universe where we do not belong, changes the system. And the changes are cumulative."

"Meaning what?" McCoy asked.

"Our warp engines normally function at a particular frequency, a frequency built into the system by the dilithium crystals, the energy conduits, and hundreds of other components. They are all tuned by nature to their universe of origin—our home universe. If the changes I speak of did not occur, we might reasonably expect that the natural frequency of the warp engines would resonate most strongly with our home universe, a universe that vibrates at the same frequency. However, because the changes between universes are cumulative, the natural frequency at which our warp engines run does not guarantee or even suggest the engines will take us home."

"We'll have to retune them," Kirk said. In his present condition the very idea seemed overwhelming, like being asked to push boulders.

"Indeed, Captain. And every time we translate from one universe to another it will be necessary for me to start over again computing the correct frequency. The more universes we travel through, the more computing will be necessary at each stage. The warp frequency needed is a function of where we begin as well as of where we wish to terminate."

"Must you use that word?" McCoy demanded. He evidently did not expect an answer, because he went to see how Payton was doing. He ran a medical scanner over her and said, "She'll probably sleep for a few hours." He rubbed his eyes. "We all should sleep for a few hours."

"Do the calculations," Kirk said.

Spock said, "In my present state, even assuming that hallucinations would not lead me astray, I would not finish in time. Mr. Scott and I working together would not finish in time. The monitor's computer has neither the speed nor the memory to make a significant difference."

"And without sensors the ship's computer is useless."

"For this purpose, yes."

"Then we must go back through the Aleph now."

"The probability of our finding a more favorable universe is not high."

"If we jump, we may die. If we stay here, we'll die for sure. Given the alternatives, I prefer to take a chance." Kirk struggled to his feet and went to an intercom. "Kirk to bridge. Mr. Chekov, set course for the Aleph."

"Captain?"

"The Aleph, Mr. Chekov."

"Aye, Captain."

Kirk imagined Chekov and Sulu trading speculative glances. The entire bridge crew would feel the lift that came with a dangerous but valiant attempt. No doubt they were glad to be doing something besides just sitting at their stations.

"Take us home, Jim," McCoy said.

"I'll do the best I can," Kirk said.

It was anybody's guess whether his best would be good enough. Their chances of striking the correct universe were literally an infinity to one. Not good odds in anybody's book. Their chances of jumping to a universe at least as bad as this one were better, a fact that Kirk did not find comforting.

But any chance they had was better than their chances of living in this universe, which were a flat zero. Besides, they did not need to get home to stay alive; they needed only to find a more compatible universe, and there must be plenty of those—at least as many as there were *less* compatible universes. Must be. He did not want to ask Spock's opinion. A compatible universe would at least give Spock and Scotty and the computer time to calculate the proper warp engine frequency. Time was what they needed most. Kirk was gambling for it in the only game in town.

He gritted his teeth. Merely staying alive was not enough. The *Enterprise* must return to its home universe in order to stop Omen. The death of Starfleet was too high a price to pay for an uncertain and probably temporary peace. Besides, it was clear to Kirk that the imposition of peace was just another kind of war. For all his fine talk, Omen was really no better than the people he wanted to stop.

Kirk and Spock boarded a turbolift. It groaned with the effort of carrying them, and the lights dimmed once. As dangerous as it was, Kirk did not regret his decision. They had to leave now, or they probably would never leave. They would deal with the next universe when they came to it.

Kirk took a deep breath as the turbolift doors opened. With a great effort he strode to his seat and said, "Report, Mr. Chekov."

"Course to Aleph laid in, sir."

"Main screen, Uhura."

The screen came to life and showed them the Aleph. Kirk looked past its edge, hoping that would save him from mentally falling into it. Should he use the warp engines or not? Either way, Kirk knew the probabilities were not in their favor. Spock couldn't help him. Kirk would have to go with his guts.

"Mr. Sulu, take us through. Full impulse power."

"Aye, Captain."

Kirk could feel the strain on the impulse engines, and with body English he tried to help. The ship approached the Aleph, and Kirk saw a multitude of things, many of which he could not identify. The Aleph seemed to open and open, revealing more and more bits of the universe, and then the ship was through.

Everyone but Spock cheered when they saw the stars. Spock only raised an eyebrow and nodded. For him that would serve for a cheer.

"We made it, Spock," Kirk cried. He felt better already. And he must not have been kidding himself about his sudden vitality, because the impulse engines sounded normal, too.

"Perhaps, Captain. Many universes must have stars."

"McCoy to bridge. Did we make it home, Jim?"

Kirk said, "There still seems to be some question about that, Doctor. I'll get back to you." Without navigational sensors, and unless they had incredibly good luck, doing a star-by-star match would be impossible. He looked at Spock and said, "But at least we have time."

Kirk felt better with each passing minute. Though he did not know whether or not they were in their home universe, he was encouraged by the fact that the very nature of this universe was not hostile. The combination of renewed good health and a stretch of useful time made him optimistic. He felt like singing, but he was not a singing man.

"Yes, Captain. I will begin." Spock stood and

walked toward the turbolift but was stopped by what he saw on the viewscreen.

Kirk turned to look at what had so surprised Spock. He stiffened, and the smile fell off his face.

On the viewscreen before them was a Klingon warship.

Chapter Eleven

"I NEED SENSORS NOW, Mr. Scott," Kirk cried into the intercom.

"We're working as fast as we can down here, sir," Scotty said. He didn't mind pushing himself and his people, but Kirk knew that Scott hated mistreating his machines.

"Now, Mr. Scott," Kirk said.

"Aye, sir. You'll have them."

Kirk studied the Klingon ship. At first he decided that by the greatest good fortune they had leapt into their home universe after all. Then he noticed details on the Klingon ship that caused him to question his first determination. For one thing, he'd never seen a Klingon ship with the main sensor painted a dusty rose. The triform symbol of the Klingon empire was missing from the warp pylons, replaced by a simple

162

diagram of a single circling planet, or what might have been a hydrogen atom. The shape of the disrupter cannon was slightly different from what he recalled. What, if anything, did all these small differences add up to?

Just beyond the Klingon ship the Aleph fulminated. Would the Klingons let them at it? The Klingons that Kirk knew would not allow the *Enterprise* to pass without a fight, and yet Kirk was not ready to throw the first punch until he had more information about these particular Klingons and their faintly peculiar ship. Maybe throwing a punch would not even be necessary. He swallowed and said, "Hail them, Lieutenant."

"Captain, they're hailing us. But they're not using a standard communication channel or a standard hail."

After what he'd seen, Kirk was not surprised. "Not nasty enough, eh, Lieutenant? Put it on the screen. And see if you can sweet-talk Mr. Scott into giving me some sensors."

Uhura didn't even try to hide her smile when she said, "Yes, sir," and she moved to comply.

The picture of the Klingon ship was replaced by what must have been the ship's captain. Kirk goggled.

The first unusual thing he noticed about the Klingon was that he didn't seem to be angry. He seemed more—Kirk searched for the right word—surprised. The Klingon's uniform was also different from what Kirk had come to expect. Instead of a severe and sinister outfit of darkly colored leather and rough cloth, this Klingon was wearing a costume of thin flowing stuff that was a pastel green. Lace crossed one shoulder and suspended a fringe of gemlike red teardrops. The Klingon gaped at Kirk and said something incomprehensible.

"What is that, Uhura, some Klingon dialect?"

Uhura said, "I'm familiar with a few of the Klingon dialects, sir. This doesn't sound like any of them."

"Renegades, Spock?"

"Unknown, Captain."

"Lieutenant, put the universal translator on line."

"Aye, sir."

Kirk said, "This is Captain James T. Kirk of the Federation starship *Enterprise*. Please identify yourself."

Seemingly near hysteria, the Klingon captain shrieked something. The translator could make nothing of it.

Kirk said, "We are on a peaceful mission. Please identify yourself." Kirk knew that what he said probably meant no more to the Klingon than what the Klingon words meant to him, but Kirk hoped that his tone of voice would calm the Klingon, convince him, at least momentarily, that his intentions were not belligerent.

The Klingon spoke again, but this time he wasn't hysterical. Of course, he wasn't angry either, which was what Kirk would have expected under these circumstances. The Klingon seemed more petulant, like a fussing child. It didn't matter. The universal translator needed samples to work from, and Kirk was provoking the Klingon into giving them samples. The Klingon continued to speak. Occasional words came through, but not yet enough to give Kirk even the gist of the conversation.

Payton stepped down next to Kirk, and he said, "I see that you escaped Dr. McCoy."

"He let me go. He couldn't find anything wrong with me. Can I help?" She appraised what was on the screen.

"Not unless you're an expert on rare Klingon dialects."

"We have partial sensors," Spock said quietly.

The Klingon stopped speaking and looked at Kirk expectantly. Kirk held up an open palm in what he hoped was a universal gesture of peace and said, "Is it a Klingon ship, Spock?"

"We know very little about the internal design of Klingon ships, but the exterior is within ten percent of known norms for the Kreega class."

"Ten percent. That's rather a wide deviation, isn't it?"

"For a military vessel, yes."

"Armament?"

"Impossible to say at this time. Sensors detect various structures and power usage curves with which I am unfamiliar, but they follow the general Klingon pattern for deflectors and weapons."

Kirk liked to know what he was tangling with, but it seemed not to be. He said, "What about the crew? Are they Klingons?"

"As far as I am able to determine. We are not yet capable of making a full sensor scan."

Evidently the translator had digested enough of the language, because when the Klingon spoke again, Kirk understood.

"Who are you? The planet is ours. Please go away."

"I never heard a Klingon say 'please'," said Uhura with some amazement.

Neither had Kirk, but at the moment he was more interested in the planet the Klingons claimed than he was in their etiquette. If the planet was on the *Enterprise* books, it would tell them where they were. Again Kirk said, "This is Captain James T. Kirk of the Federation starship *Enterprise*. Please identify yourself."

The Klingon said, "I am Captain Iola of the Klingee Association. We know of no Federation."

Kirk was certain that giving Iola the textbook description of the Federation would do none of them any good. He said, "We are part of a partnership of space explorers, like yourselves."

"We are the only space explorers. The planet is ours. Please go away." That seemed to conclude the matter for Iola.

Kirk asked, "What do you mean, 'only space explorers'?"

"Don't be stupid," Iola said. "We are the only ones because there are no others. The Klingee are the masters of all, from our home planet to Kardoma's Wall at the end of the universe, beyond which no man sees."

"A moment, Captain," Kirk said, and he gave Uhura the signal to cut off the outgoing audio. He leaned on the rail around the upper level of the bridge and asked, "What do you think, Spock? Are they just bragging, or what?"

"It is possible that they overstate their own position, Captain, but the Klingee's uniqueness in this universe would explain much: their speech patterns, their manner of dress, their attitude toward us, and their dusty-rose sensor."

"Then they have no combat experience."

"Perhaps not. Perhaps they fight one another. Humans fought one another for centuries. However, the pattern we see here is not generally that of a militant race."

They were right back where they started, confronting an unknown enemy in an unknown universe. "What about the planet, Spock?"

Spock spoke while looking into his viewer. Blue light washed his face. He said, "We are within three standard planetary distances of it. From all indications, it is the planet Earth. Geographical features match to within one percent."

Spock's announcement shocked Kirk, and for a moment he could not speak. He wet his lips and said, "The Klingons—er, Klingees—have conquered Earth?"

"Perhaps, Captain, but not in the usual sense. Sensors read plant life and some simple animal forms. No artificial structures, no electromagnetic radiation other than the planet's natural magnetic field, and no chemicals in the air to indicate industry of any technical level."

"Humans never evolved?"

"Evidently. Nor any other creature."

Despite Spock's assurances, something in Kirk wanted to save this Earth. That the Klingons—Klingees—should exploit it seemed obscene. And yet, Kirk told himself, what the Klingees did with the planet below did not matter. There were no Earth people to harm.

Perhaps a more important interpretation of Spock's discovery was that the *Enterprise* could not possibly be in its home universe. And Klingees were certainly not Klingons. Kirk hoped that the differences would be in their favor. So far, it seemed to be the case.

Captain Iola said, "What are you talking about? I demand to know."

Kirk nodded at Uhura and said to the screen, "We have no interest in the planet. But we must have free access to that whirling body behind you."

"That's ours, too," Iola said. "Everything is ours. It's all ours."

"We'll see about that," Kirk grumbled. He was not impressed with what he'd seen of the Klingees so far. They had a ship, and probably weapons, but he doubted if they'd had much combat training. Even if they fought among themselves, it could not be much of a contest. Still, Kirk did not like to shoot first and ask questions later. He said, "Captain Iola, our need of the whirling body is only temporary."

"That does not matter. It's ours, and you can't have it." The screen went blank and a moment later showed the Klingee ship again.

"We're dealing with children," Payton said softly to Kirk.

Kirk nodded. The Klingee were bullies, used to having their way. Maybe, like bullies, they could be frightened by a show of force where they expected none. He said, "Let's see how the lords of creation react to a challenge. Mr. Chekov, fire a low-energy phaser burst across the bow of the Klingee ship."

"Aye, Captain."

"Fire when ready."

The phasers warbled as the needle of brilliant light shot out, narrowly missing the Klingee ship.

Captain Iola's voice came over the audio channel. "You shouldn't have done that. You'll be sorry now."

Spock said, "Radical change of power usage aboard the Klingee ship. I believe they are readying a weapon."

Kirk barely had time to call for shields when a spiral of orange fire twisted toward the *Enterprise*. The spiral struck with a loud gonging and caused the ship to heave when the inertial compensators were momentarily overloaded. Stars whirled across the viewscreen, and Kirk closed his eyes against the dizziness he felt.

"Full impulse," Kirk commanded. The damned thing must have grabbed the ship and flung it away like a big, flat stone.

"Helm won't answer," Sulu cried.

Kirk had to stop the ship from spinning out of control, and he called for microsteering verniers. These were capable of making only small but very precise adjustments and were generally used only for maneuvering in and around spacedock. They were on an entirely different control system than the free space helm.

The stars slowed to a casual drift. A gabble of damage reports came in.

"Uhura?" Kirk asked.

"Minor damage all over the ship. A lot of bumps and bruises. Dr. McCoy doesn't sound happy."

Kirk smiled. At any minute McCoy would charge

up there complaining about how he ran the ship. After catching his breath Kirk called into the intercom, "What's going on down there, Mr. Scott?"

"Whatever hit us knocked out primary helm control."

"Can you repair it?"

"This time, Captain. Another shock like that and we might not be so lucky." Kirk had to prevent the Klingee from attacking again. Of course, they might have no intention of attacking again, but did a bully ever quit while he was ahead? He said, "Soon, Mr. Scott."

"Aye."

"Can you tell us where we are, Spock?"

"Aye, Captain. Local constellations are within two percent of resembling the formations around the planet Earth in our universe. We were thrown approximately five hundred thousand kilometers."

Half a million kilometers was not far compared to interstellar distances, but it might as well be parsecs if the *Enterprise* couldn't navigate back to the Aleph. Kirk reconsidered the Klingees. Evidently they had a weapon that no one at home, not even the Klingons, had yet perfected. However, if the Klingees had it, the Klingons might be close to perfecting it even now. One more reason they had to get home: to warn the Federation about the Klingons' possible new weapon.

"Message coming in from the Klingees, Captain."

"On screen."

The starfield on screen was replaced by the smirking face of Captain Iola. "I guess we showed you, Captain James T. Kirk. You better not come back here, either.

Our fleet will arrive soon, and it'll take care of you permanently."

"Captain—" Kirk said.

"No more talking. Stay away or we'll use our cyclor on you again." The starfield returned to the screen.

"What do you make of that, Spock?"

"Only the obvious. They are threatening us to keep us away from their property."

"If they have that cyclor of theirs, why do they need the fleet?"

"Unknown, Captain."

Kirk shook his head. There was no better straight-line thinker than Mr. Spock, but he had little talent for deviousness. Kirk said, "I've suggested that you take up poker, Mr. Spock."

"I assume your comment has some bearing on our current situation."

"You may so assume."

Spock shrugged and said, "I derive sufficient amusement from three-dimensional chess. It is a game of logic and skill. Poker is a game of chance."

"Yes, but poker can teach us lessons that three-dimensional chess cannot. Such as why the Klingees need the fleet."

"Indeed, Captain?"

"Yes. I think they're bluffing. I think that the cyclor is either a one-shot weapon or a weapon that takes time to build up a charge before it can be used again. The Klingees want to make sure we don't attack before their fleet arrives because they cannot defend themselves. A fleet would give them an acceptable margin of protection. What do you think?"

"It is a viable theory," Spock admitted. "We might test it by attacking them again and observing their response."

"And risk the ship. If I'm wrong, we could permanently lose our ability to navigate. I have a better idea. Ms. Payton points out that the Klingees are like children."

"Human children."

"Yes, Mr. Spock, human children. I suggest that we can frighten them away, Iola's ship and the entire fleet, if we convince them that we are too powerful to fight, all-powerful."

"Perhaps," said Spock. "The problem will be in convincing them."

"I don't think so. Using the Aleph, we can see literally everything in the universe, maybe in all universes. Surely I can discover a secret aboard Iola's ship that they think we have no way of knowing."

"Given the little we know of Klingee psychology, such a plan might work. But I must insist that I be the one to search the Aleph for the secret."

"Keeping all the fun for yourself, Spock?"

Spock frowned. The man couldn't take a joke. Or he was determined to pretend that he didn't know a joke when he saw one. "No, Captain. As a Vulcan, I am the only crew member on the *Enterprise* who has the mental discipline to maintain his own identity while looking into the Aleph, and therefore the only one who has any chance of completing the mission. The fact is, sir, that we cannot afford to lose you."

"You won't lose me."

"The probability of your completing the mission is

less than one in three thousand. The chance that your psychological makeup will be permanently impaired is much greater."

Where did Spock get these numbers? Did the recitation of probabilities constitute Vulcan humor? Numbers with a three in them are funny? Kirk said, "I'm not asking for your permission, Spock."

Spock pressed his lips together. Kirk knew he didn't want to argue with his captain, but as first officer, Spock felt it was his duty to point out all likely dangers. Moreover, Kirk knew that Spock was probably correct. Payton had not been able to maintain her sense of self for long, and even Spock had had difficulty. The truth was that Kirk was curious. He wanted to abandon himself to the Aleph, experience it fully. He felt that he would never have a better chance. And yet Spock *was* probably right.

Kirk said, "Let's compromise, Spock. I'll search the Aleph, and you can stay with me the whole time, pull me back if I seem to have gone too far."

Spock considered that, eyebrows up. "Very well, Captain. And Dr. McCoy can do the same for Ms. Payton."

Payton nodded.

Kirk said, "We have sensors now. Do we need Ms. Payton?"

Spock said, "In their present condition, ship's sensors are not sufficient to study the Aleph from this distance. Therefore, while you watch Ms. Payton's monitor, it is necessary that Ms. Payton once again watch the main viewscreen. Her implant will send the image down to Professor Omen's equipment, and then to her monitor."

Kirk had not counted on Payton's involvement. "What about the records of the Aleph we made?"

"Not sufficiently detailed for our purpose."

"Very well," Kirk said, resigned to putting Payton through the mill once again.

"I will make the proper adjustments to Ms. Payton's monitor," Spock said, and he left the bridge.

"Doesn't give an inch, does he?" Payton asked.

"His stubbornness," Kirk said, "is both his pride and his curse."

Kirk sat in the chair before Payton's monitor, amused by McCoy's discomfort.

"So you're going to take a look for yourself," McCoy said mournfully.

"You act as if I'm about to die, Doctor."

"I just don't want to lose you in there."

"Mr. Spock is my guardian angel. You will be ministering to Ms. Payton. She's on the bridge waiting for you."

To Spock McCoy said, "Pull him away if he sinks too deep. I'll do the same with Ms. Payton."

"Understood, Doctor."

"Get out of here, Bones. We're wasting time. We don't know when that Klingee fleet will arrive."

After a last worried look at Kirk McCoy left.

"He's as bad as you are," Kirk said.

"We are both"—Spock searched for a word—"concerned."

"I appreciate that. Let's get started."

Presently the monitor showed the face of Lieutenant Uhura. She was saying, "No, actually being communications officer is more than just answering the

174

phone. It can be very exciting." The view swung around when McCoy came in through the turbolift and he said, "They're ready down there, Ms. Payton. How about you?" Kirk watched through Payton's eyes as McCoy conducted her to the command chair. Kirk had seen the bridge thousands of times under many conditions, and yet, watching it on the monitor screen, he was fascinated, as if he'd never seen it before.

Spock pushed a button on the desk intercom and said, "Ms. Payton, you may begin."

"Let's see the Aleph, Uhura," Payton said.

The stars shifted, and a prick of bright light appeared in the middle of the monitor screen. It was the Aleph. Spock made an adjustment and brought the image of the Aleph closer. Being a point, it increased only in intensity, not in size.

Spock said, "Concentrate, Captain. It is the only sure way to success."

"I'll be fine, Spock."

For the first time Kirk gave himself up to the Aleph entirely. He saw the face of every crew member on the *Enterprise*, the contents of their closets (enough to make a captain blush), the harsh and nervous dazzle inside the warp engines, the lattice structure of dilithium crystals, and individual dilithium molecules. He tried to shift his point of view to the Klingee ship, where he could find something hidden, something private and unknowable.

He lost the sense of his chair, and then of his own body. He felt his self-awareness lighten and diffuse from a near-tangible thing to a dissipating cloud. Kirk tried to catch the edges of the cloud, to keep it confined, but with less success as time went on. And soon holding the cloud in the bowl of his consciousness didn't matter. He took in everything the Aleph showed him, without prejudice, without selectivity, without question. And soon after that the visions in the Aleph were all that existed.

Spock stood next to Kirk's chair, looking only at him. At this time he could not afford to fall into the Aleph himself. Kirk's eyes were open, staring, sucking in the image of the Aleph.

"What is your condition, Captain?" Spock asked.

"I am everywhere."

The answer did not assure Spock overmuch, but the fact that the captain could answer at all was encouraging.

The sound of the bosun's whistle came from the intercom, followed by the voice of Lieutenant Uhura. "Bridge to Captain Kirk."

"Spock here. The captain is unavailable."

"You'd better get up here, Mr. Spock. The Klingee fleet is closing on us."

"I will be there momentarily, Lieutenant. Spock out."

Spock had two alternatives. He could pull Kirk out now, or he could command the bridge himself. Judging by Ms. Payton's condition after her first session, the captain would need at least an hour's rest after being pulled out of the Aleph. Spock's only logical choice was to go to the bridge now. After all, his first duty was to the ship. That had been true even when his father's life hung in the balance. Yet Spock could not leave the captain alone.

"Spock to Nurse Chapel."

"Here, Mr. Spock."

"Please attend to Captain Kirk. He is in Ms. Payton's cabin. Enter without announcing yourself. If he is drawn too deeply into the Aleph, you must extract him immediately. And I must stress that under no circumstances are you to look at the Aleph yourself."

"Yes, Mr. Spock. But what if—"

Spock knew that his instructions were vague, insufficient for the situation. He would have to trust what had been called Chapel's "maternal instincts." Spock said, "I have no time, Nurse. I will be on the bridge if you need me."

"Yes, Mr. Spock." She still sounded unsure.

Spock punched off the intercom and left hurriedly for the bridge.

Chapter Twelve

KIRK AWOKE. He was himself again, and yet an odd discomfort remained, one that he'd never experienced before. He felt as if his consciousness were limited somehow, enclosed. As if, psychologically, he were living inside an egg.

He opened his eyes and looked at the ceiling. It was much like every other ceiling aboard the *Enterprise*. Behind him was a familiar slow, rhythmic sound. What was that sound? His heartbeat. No, not his heartbeat, but an electronic representation of it. He must be on a diagnostic couch in sickbay.

He called out, "Bones," and he was aware that he'd made no sound. He'd called out only in his head. He tried again and succeeded only in making a sound like a frog.

Then McCoy was standing over him, waving his

scanner as if it were a magic wand. "You just lie there, Jim. Spock has everything under control."

What needed to be under control? Had the Klingee fleet arrived? Had it attacked? Kirk croaked again.

"You'll be catching flies any minute, Captain. Rest. That's doctor's orders."

Kirk was going to argue with McCoy, but he lost track of what he was going to say. The next thing he knew, he jerked awake. Until then he wasn't even aware that he'd fallen asleep. After he was awake he remembered that he'd dreamed about the Aleph. Only in his dream, instead of seeing the pieces of the universe with sharp clarity, he saw them as revealed through swirling holes in a thick, ominous fog.

He opened his eyes and saw Nurse Chapel standing over him, a concerned expression on her face. Maybe she would answer some questions. He swallowed and found his throat sleeved with sandpaper. He swallowed again. Better. Kirk meant to ask what was going on but managed to bleat only the first word.

"When Mr. Spock went to the bridge I watched you until Dr. McCoy called me. I made sure you hadn't swallowed your tongue and then got you down to sickbay as quickly as I could."

If Spock had left him in Chapel's care without taking time to fully explain what Kirk was doing, maybe the Klingee fleet really had arrived. He had to get up to the bridge. While he struggled to sit up, Chapel, the traitor, called McCoy. Before McCoy arrived Kirk noticed that Payton was sleeping on the couch next to him. Poor kid; she probably hadn't bargained for this kind of abuse when she'd had that implant installed.

McCoy rushed in and pushed Kirk back onto the couch. "You'd never make it across the room, let alone all the way to the bridge."

"Spock—"

"Spock told me to tell you that the Klingee fleet arrived, but it seems more interested in that empty Earth than in the *Enterprise*. The ship is in no danger."

That was good news, if it was true. Spock wouldn't lie, but McCoy might, to keep him in bed. And Spock would know McCoy might. Even if the report was true, Kirk knew that the situation could change in seconds. He tried to sit up again. McCoy called, "Nurse, bring me the really large anesthetic mallet."

Kirk knew that McCoy was kidding about the mallet, but he also knew that McCoy would fill him full of sedatives if he didn't cooperate. Kirk said, "I want to see Spock."

After a moment of consideration McCoy relented and called the bridge. A few minutes later Spock stood next to Kirk's couch and said, "I trust you are well, Captain."

"I feel like a ghost inside my own body."

"It'll pass," McCoy said. "It did with Payton."

Neither Spock nor McCoy volunteered any more information. They watched him as if they expected him to evaporate at any moment. Perhaps they were just being kind, not wanting to rush his recovery, but their actions made Kirk tense and impatient. He asked, "How's the ship?"

"We can now navigate. And Mr. Scott progresses with his sensor repairs."

"We still have partial sensors?"

"Yes."

"That's something, I guess. What about the Klingee fleet?"

"The fleet seems to have no particular interest in the *Enterprise* as long as it does not approach the Aleph or the planet."

"You experimented?"

"Aye, Captain. None of the Klingee paid the least attention to the *Enterprise* until, on my command, we approached the Aleph at one quarter impulse."

"And then?"

"Captain Iola warned us away. I chose to take his threat seriously."

"Prudent, Mr. Spock. But the result is we still don't have anything with which to impress the Klingee."

"No. However, my time has been well spent. Using my own observations and the recordings made by Ms. Payton's monitor, I have made progress toward finding a proper formula for retuning the warp engines."

"I thought the recordings didn't have enough detail to be useful."

"Not useful for spying, Captain, but they do suggest certain facts about the geometry of the small dimensions, facts I found very useful indeed."

Leave it to Spock to get blood from a turnip. Kirk asked, "How close are you?"

"Very close. But once I am finished, Mr. Scott will need nearly an hour to adjust the engines to my specifications. By normal engineering standards the specifications are rather bizarre."

"Mr. Scott won't be happy."

"I am aware of that, Captain."

Kirk sat up, and McCoy moved toward him as if Kirk were made of glass and in danger of falling to the floor. "I'm all right, Bones." He looked at Spock and went on, "But if we can't get to the Aleph, all of your work will have been for nothing."

"Indeed, Captain. If every one of the Klingee ships is armed with a cyclor—and I have no reason to believe they are not—then the *Enterprise* is hardly a match for the fleet."

"If we can't outfight them, we'll have to outthink them."

"Mr. Kent won't be happy," Ms. Payton said.

Kirk and Spock looked at her. Kirk had forgotten she was there. She was sitting up with her legs dangling over the edge of the couch. McCoy ran a scanner over her and said, "The machine says you're feeling fine. What do you say?"

She smiled and said, "Who am I to argue with the machine?"

Spock said, "Despite Ms. Payton's apparent fitness, I hesitate to ask her to look deeply into the Aleph for a third time."

Payton bit her bottom lip and frowned, but she said nothing.

Kirk said, "I would be delighted to consider an alternative."

Spock looked at Payton and shook his head. "I have none. I am sorry."

Payton shrugged and said, "That's all right, Mr. Spock. I don't think it hit me quite so hard the second time."

"Bones?"

"It hit you hard enough, Ms. Payton. Captain, you can't put this woman's life in danger again. Why not use those partial sensors of yours?"

Spock said, "They are only partial sensors, Doctor, and not capable of taking in the great volumes of information required for our search to be meaningful."

"There must be some alternative," McCoy said.

Spock said, "The captain asked for suggestions. Unless you have one, we must proceed as planned."

Kirk nodded and said, "Ms. Payton, if Conrad Franklin Kent fires you, I think we can find a place for you in Starfleet."

Payton said, "Thank you, I guess," but she was smiling when she said it. The woman had a lot of charm. Once again Kirk was sorry that she was spoken for.

When Kirk began to get up McCoy tried to stop him again. But Kirk said, "If Ms. Payton is going to risk her life one more time, the least I can do is take my post on the bridge."

McCoy could see that he was fighting a losing battle. He said, "All right. I'll be along after I tie up some loose ends here. All of you be careful."

Spock stared at McCoy for a moment, single eyebrow raised. Kirk only said that they'd do their best. Payton kissed McCoy on the cheek, which pleased him for a moment, and then he remembered how upset he was, and he merely seemed confused. As they left sickbay Kirk thanked Chapel for saving him from the Aleph. She seemed a little puzzled about what had actually happened but was willing to accept the gratitude.

As Kirk, Spock, and Payton walked to the turbolift Kirk said, "You were right, Spock. The Aleph sucked me right out through my eyes."

The truth was, even now Kirk was not entirely comfortable inside his own skin. Everything he saw looked familiar, not just because he'd walked along this corridor many times before, but because he'd seen it and thousands of other corridors in the Aleph. Because of the Aleph his memory was deeper, more profound. In his mind, briefly, for no more time than a star takes to twinkle once, this corridor between sickbay and the turbolift became the archetype, the fundamental model for all corridors.

And then, though the profundity was gone as quickly as it had come, the memory of what he'd seen in the Aleph remained. He remembered not only the corridor itself, but the electronics buried in it and the electrons flowing through the electronics, living pricks of light always in a hurry; he knew the nearly invisible nick in the intercom button at the corridor's intersection; the microscopic layer of organic molecules laid down against the wall by the respiration of his crew; the excited atoms in the glow bars in the ceiling.

And when crew members passed Kirk knew them, too, and what they kept in their closets, and how some of them picked at their fingers when they were alone, or pulled their ears, or rubbed their chins. He had seen everything in the Aleph, and when he saw something in life it reminded him of the millions of other events or actions or artifacts like it or around it, reminded him as if it were something he had experienced but forgotten till now.

"The Aleph *is* engaging, Captain."

"It's damned hypnotic." Kirk smiled ruefully. "I wonder if anything will ever again surprise me."

"It all looks familiar, doesn't it?" Payton commented.

"Henry the Fifth," Spock said.

"What?" Kirk and Payton said together.

"Henry the Fifth, by your Earth playwright Shakespeare. I quote:

> *". . . Can this cockpit hold*
> *The vasty fields of France? Or may we cram*
> *Within this wooden O the very casques*
> *That did affright the air at Agincourt?"*

Kirk said, "The Aleph is Shakespeare's wooden O? I suppose so, if we allow for poetry."

Payton had been staring at Spock ever since he'd mentioned Shakespeare. Now she said, "I had no idea that Vulcans had an interest in the arts."

"We are generally self-conscious dancers, Ms. Payton, but in the other arts the Vulcans' love of logic does not preclude our appreciation of beauty."

The turbolift came, and they walked aboard. The captain said, "Deck 5," and the lift began to whine. It arrived at Deck 5, and Kirk put a hand on Spock's arm. He said, "Be careful, Spock. At the moment you're the most valuable officer I have."

Spock jerked around as if Kirk had succeeded in surprising him. "I, sir?"

"Among the crews on the ships that have disappeared, you're the only Vulcan science officer. That gives the *Enterprise* a chance not enjoyed by the other ships Omen sent through the Aleph. You're the only one with enough mental discipline to remember your mission while inside the Aleph. The *Enterprise* could never get out of this without you."

"May I remind you, sir, that we are not 'out of this' yet?"

"No. But we will be."

"Wishful thinking, Captain?"

"No, Mr. Spock. Trust. Trust in you and Ms. Payton and in the *Enterprise*."

"I will endeavor to be worthy."

"Me, too," said Payton.

Spock hurried off to Ms. Payton's cabin while Kirk and Payton rose the few decks to the bridge. Kirk wondered who he was kidding, or if he was kidding anybody. Even Vulcans liked to be appreciated, but neither Spock nor Payton needed a pep talk. Both of them understood the importance of what they were trying to do.

Spock's presence did in fact improve their chances of getting home, but it did not guarantee that they would. There were many factors to consider, and certainly factors they knew nothing about. He trusted his people, believed in them, but they were not magicians.

On the main viewscreen Kirk saw a planet that was not Earth—not their Earth, anyway; a single twinkling light that had to be the Aleph—too far away to be either useful or dangerous; and the Klingee fleet arrayed in what he assumed was a battle formation.

Or maybe the pattern just satisfied their esthetics. Considering the little he knew about them, either guess could be correct. In any case, he counted only fifteen ships. He wondered if that was the entire fleet. It didn't matter. If they were armed with cyclors, fifteen was more than enough. He tried to identify Iola's ship but couldn't. Every Klingee ship had a dusty-rose main sensor.

McCoy came onto the bridge and without a word went to stand next to Ms. Payton. She was sitting in Spock's chair rubbing her palms on her legs and biting her lower lip. Kirk hated putting her through this again, but even Spock admitted that using Payton's enhanced senses was the only way for them to get the look at the Aleph they needed.

"Mr. Spock is signaling ready, sir," Uhura said.

"Very well. Ms. Payton?" He looked over his shoulder.

"Ready, Captain," Payton said. McCoy nodded.

Kirk said, "Mr. Sulu, give the *Enterprise* a nudge toward the Aleph. Let's see how close we can get without alarming somebody."

"Aye, sir."

Very slowly the planet and the fleet moved to one side of the screen, and the Aleph grew brighter in the center.

"Message coming in, sir."

"All stop. On screen, Uhura."

A Klingee Kirk had not seen before appeared. He was dressed in some flimsy blue stuff, and he had more droplet-shaped jewels dangling from his shoulder lace than did Iola.

The Klingee said, "I am Ruho, commander of the Klingee fleet. The spinning thing is ours. The planet is ours. Go away, or we will use the cyclor again."

Kirk wondered if any of them had actually looked at the Aleph, or if they were concentrating on the planet. Could their brains comprehend what they saw in the Aleph even as well as humans did? Maybe as far as they were concerned the Aleph was just a "spinning thing."

"Do we have magnification?" Kirk asked.

"We do, sir," said Sulu, "but only up to magnification three."

Kirk wished Scott would hurry. A starship without full sensors was like a blind man with his hands tied behind his back. "Magnification three, then."

They were some thousands of kilometers closer to the Aleph than they had been before. Perhaps they could get even closer, but Kirk didn't want to push the Klingee now, with their plan ready. "Would you like to sit closer to the screen, Ms. Payton?"

"I'm fine, Captain."

"All right. Any time you're ready."

Nothing much happened on the bridge for a while. Kirk went up to help McCoy keep watch over Payton. She quickly fell into the trancelike state that characterized someone studying the Aleph. Bridge machinery boinked and hummed and twittered. Crew members concentrated on their boards and shuffled their feet. Kirk didn't know what he would do if Payton dived too deep before Spock told them he'd located what he was looking for. He hoped he would not have to find out.

Time passed slowly. When Mr. Spock's call came

Kirk was certain that hours had passed. That was not possible, of course. McCoy turned Payton away from the Aleph, and she collapsed. He called for orderlies and a stretcher.

"I'll see how Spock is doing," Kirk said.

McCoy promised to come up after he got Payton settled. "Not even Spock's Vulcan constitution can stand much of this." The orderlies arrived as Kirk left.

Kirk found Spock with his head down on the desk in front of Payton's equipment. He immediately sat up straight when Kirk entered. "Are you all right, Spock?" Kirk asked.

"I am fatigued. It will pass."

"I want McCoy to have a look at you."

"It is unnecessary."

"He'll be here soon. Wait for him. That's an order."

Spock gave a small nod, as if nodding were a great effort.

"You found what we were looking for."

Spock said, "I believe so," and he told Kirk all about it. Kirk agreed that it would do the trick. Neither of them was certain, of course; guessing what an alien would find valuable or embarrassing was difficult, but Spock and Kirk had dealt with many kinds of beings, and their guess was an educated one. Or at least an experienced one. The very fact that they knew of this object's existence might be all that was necessary to frighten Captain Iola.

"Did you finish the formula?"

"I did. The answer is surprisingly simple. The mathematics allows many components to cancel."

"All the better. After McCoy sees you, get it to Mr. Scott and tell him to start tuning the warp engines immediately. If our plan works, I want us into the Aleph and away before the Klingee have second thoughts about our omnipotence."

"Understood, Captain." With difficulty Spock stood.

Once more Kirk was about to order Spock to wait for McCoy when the bosun's whistle came over the intercom and Mr. Scott's voice said, "Engineering to Captain Kirk."

"Kirk here, Scotty. What is it?"

"You have the full range of sensors, Captain."

"Well done, Mr. Scott. Mr. Spock will be down in a few minutes with some unorthodox tune-up specifications. Please follow them exactly."

"Exactly how unorthodox, sir?" Scott asked suspiciously.

"Mr. Spock will discuss that with you."

"Aye, Captain." Scott did not sound happy, but he could be counted on to implement Spock's instructions.

McCoy came in looking worried.

"How is she, Bones?"

"She'll live, but that last bout was much more difficult for her than she pretended. I wouldn't be surprised if she slept for a few days."

"See that she gets all the rest she needs. We have sensors now. She won't have to do it again."

McCoy studied Spock with critical detachment and said, "For a Vulcan he looks positively decrepit."

"Thank you, Doctor. Is that a professional opinion?"

"No. That was just a friendly observation. The professional opinion comes *after* the examination."

"Hurry up, Bones. Spock has to get down to engineering."

McCoy ran some scanners over Spock and pronounced him fit, but ready for a long nap. "Vulcan physiology being what it is, he can probably go without the nap for a while."

"He'll need to, Doctor. Thank you. Come on, Spock."

Kirk and Spock went down to engineering. In the turbolift Spock sagged against the wall.

"Can you do this?" Kirk asked.

Spock stood away from the wall and clasped his hands behind his back. "I am in control, Captain."

Kirk was aware that Spock had not answered his question, but surely it would soon answer itself.

Though the Klingee were leaving them alone for the moment, that situation might change. Back in the home universe Professor Omen was making demands, sending other ships to their deaths through other Alephs. Time was their enemy just as surely as space and the geometry of small dimensions. Even so, Kirk could not ignore the suffering of his friend. He said, "If you need some time, Spock . . ."

"Captain, we must do this now, as soon as possible. My calculations are rather vague on how long an Aleph remains stable, but I believe that the one we have been traveling through is nearing the end of its life."

"Anything we can do about that?"

"The theory of small dimensions presents us with intriguing possibilities. But without further study they remain *only* possibilities."

Once again time was their enemy. They had entire

universes to play with, and yet time was limiting their choices, boxing them in.

When Kirk made no comment, Spock went on. "I suggest we work as quickly as we can. If that Aleph loses cohesion, it will tear itself apart and break up in seconds. We will be marooned in this universe."

Kirk swallowed hard. It was amazing how calm Spock could be while making these dire pronouncements. He asked, "How long do we have?"

"Hours. Perhaps less."

"We can't make another one?"

"Professor Omen is some years ahead of me in designing an Aleph generator. Reproducing his work is possible, but I would need a similar amount of time, perhaps longer."

The situation was even more desperate than Kirk had imagined. While the ship remained intact he had hope, but he'd rarely felt so cut off from civilization. He was an explorer, something of an adventurer in the mode of earlier centuries, when men sailed beyond the edge of the world in wooden ships. Satisfying one's own curiosity had its rewards, but ultimately exploration was meaningless unless one could report home.

The turbolift seemed to take forever to get to the engineering level, but it arrived at last, distracting Kirk from his gloomy thoughts. When Spock told Scotty what he had in mind Scotty went pale and said it was impossible. Spock assured him that it was not only possible but necessary.

"Aye, but it'll tie the warp engines into knots."

"Let's get to it, Mr. Scott," Kirk said.

"Aye," said Scott unhappily, but he set to work with

a will. Spock brought his calculations up onto a terminal and read off settings to Kirk and Scott. They ran from station to station, resetting controls and studying how the changes affected gauges. Scott continued to shake his head and mumble about his poor bairns.

Kirk could sympathize with Scott. After all, the *Enterprise* was his ship, too, and Scotty felt that Spock was hurting it. Kirk smiled. Sometimes, late in a party where Starfleet officers gathered, talk turned to the question of self-awareness of Constitution-class starships. Just how complex did a ship need to be before it took an interest in its surroundings, before it felt an emotional responsibility for the crew it carried? Everyone had heard unsubstantiated stories about how a ship had saved its crew, seemingly without the action of any living being.

Still, for his own peace of mind, Kirk had to believe that merely feeding the *Enterprise* unusual parameters would not hurt her or make her unhappy or please her, for that matter. Despite his rational arguments, Spock's odd settings made Kirk as nervous as they made Scotty.

When Spock was finished Scotty looked at the mish-mash of settings he and Kirk had just entered into the warp engine controls and shook his head.

Kirk said, "Wait for my command, Mr. Scott. When you get it I'll need warp speed immediately."

"Aye, Captain. If Mr. Spock's settings don't have us trotting up our own backsides, you'll have it."

While they rode up in the turbolift Kirk said, "You seem pensive, Mr. Spock."

"I am not pensive, Captain, merely thoughtful."

"You don't think my plan will work."

"I can concoct no better one. Yet your plan does seem to rely overmuch on theatrics."

"You have no confidence in my ability to play poker."

"On the contrary, Captain. My confidence in you is great. I lack only confidence in the ability of the Klingee to appreciate your efforts."

Kirk had not considered that possibility, but now that Spock had said it, Kirk feared that it might be true. But he had hope, too. And if Spock was right, hope was their only comfort.

Chapter Thirteen

KIRK AND SPOCK entered the bridge and went to their stations. Kirk studied the viewscreen. He saw the other Earth, the Klingee fleet, and the glimmer of the Aleph under the filter Uhura had put over it. Like many weapons, the Aleph had its own nasty beauty.

Feeling as if he were leaping into darkness, Kirk said, "Open a channel to Captain Iola."

"Aye, sir," said Uhura.

A moment later Iola appeared on the screen. He looked surprised and amused, like a kid who knew he had the upper hand and didn't mind flaunting his superiority. "Asking for the spinning thing again is pointless, Captain. We Klingee are heartless brutes."

Kirk doubted that. They had one good weapon and a bully's bluster. Of course, Kirk was not above using a little bluster himself. He said, "We have been patient, Iola, but our patience is at an end."

"Hah," Iola exclaimed. He smirked and crossed his arms.

"You and your fleet will depart now, or we will destroy you. To show you that we are merciful as well as powerful, we are willing to give you a demonstration of our omniscience and power."

Iola glanced to one side. He was desperate to turn around, see how the rest of the crew was taking his performance, but he dared not show that weakness. For the purposes of this discussion he had to pretend that he didn't care what anybody else thought.

Iola said, "Words can't hurt us."

"Perhaps," Kirk said coyly.

"What will you do?"

"You'll know it when you see it." Kirk made the cutthroat motion to Uhura, and Iola disappeared.

"How am I doing, Spock?" Kirk asked.

"The Klingee does seem to be intrigued."

"We're being hailed, Captain."

"Count to thirty and then open a channel."

"Aye, Captain," Uhura said with pleasure.

Half a minute later Iola appeared on the screen again. He said, "If you have words to say, say them."

"Very well. A component of your cyclor is defective."

Iola smiled and said, "You are making that up. You don't know anything about our cyclor."

"The component is a particle accelerator. It is about this size"—he held up his fist—"and has three red bumps on one end. On the other end is a long curved pipe."

"How did you know about that? Who told?"

"Nobody told. We see all." Kirk finished ominously, "And we tell all. For instance, we know about that thing in your cabin. It is small and brown."

Iola's eyes widened.

"It is soft and has lumps all over it. On top is a blue circle, and at the other end is——"

"What about the accelerator? You said it was broken." Iola was obviously more horrified by Kirk's second revelation than by his first. The small brown thing would obviously be a source of great embarrassment to Iola if his crew found out about it.

Kirk let the small brown thing ride. It had done its job. He said, "Not broken. Defective. The pipe has a microscopic crack in it. Eventually the crack will cause your cyclor to fail."

"You lie. There was no crack before. You put the crack there."

Kirk liked Iola's guess. It was a wrinkle Kirk hadn't thought of, but it made the beings aboard the *Enterprise* seem even more powerful. Kirk shrugged. "I didn't lie about the small brown thing, did I?"

The Klingee gaped at him and ended the transmission.

"Did it work?" Chekov asked.

"We'll see in a moment," Kirk said. "They need time to pass the word that their lives are open books."

"It would horrify *me,*" Sulu said.

"Teddy bear on the bed, Mr. Sulu?" Kirk asked.

"You got me, sir," Sulu said.

"There they go, Captain," Uhura said.

The fleet was leaving with, Kirk supposed, Captain

Iola's ship in the lead. They sailed under impulse power for a few seconds and then, like snapped rubber bands, disappeared into warp space.

"Set course for the Aleph, Mr. Chekov."

"Course has been laid in for hours, sir."

Kirk punched his intercom button and demanded, "Now, Mr. Scott."

"Aye."

"Ahead warp one, Mr. Sulu."

"Aye."

They approached the Aleph, it flashed around them, and then the stars returned. Kirk could not tell if they were the right stars or not.

"Spock?"

"Sensors indicate an exact match with navigational benchmarks. We are in the correct universe, and very near the spot from which we departed."

"I have subspace chatter, too, sir," Uhura said.

Kirk felt a surge of relief. Chekov and Sulu shook hands and then, like Kirk and the others, took pleasure in watching the friendly stars pour toward them.

"You did it, Spock!" Kirk said.

"Thank you, Captain, but I did not guide us home alone. Mr. Scott was of immense service, and we are fortunate that Ms. Payton and her implant were aboard."

Kirk mused on that for a moment. Scotty's usefulness was never a surprise. But Conrad Franklin Kent would certainly be chagrined if his chief aide earned a commendation from Starfleet. Payton deserved it, though, and the chagrin of Mr. Kent would be one of the benefits, as far as Kirk was concerned.

"How is it possible that we have not moved?" Chekov asked.

The paradox of the situation was striking. Kirk said, "We've been to two alien universes, but we didn't actually move much in normal terms." He turned to Spock and said, "Anything on Professor Omen's ship, *Erehwon?*"

"Nothing, Captain. But the Aleph is still with us, and our sensors are now fully functional. With your permission, I will search the Aleph for *Erehwon's* present course and speed."

Kirk knew that Spock had been through a lot lately. It was understandable that his posture was not quite so straight nor his voice so firm as usual. He asked, "Are you all right, Spock?"

"I recover rapidly, Captain. Besides, I find that looking at the Aleph through ship's sensors is not the raw experience it was when looking through Ms. Payton's monitor."

"You already looked?"

"It was necessary to test the sensors."

"I see." Kirk had to smile. "So now you intend to look over Omen's shoulder at his navigational telltales."

"Yes, sir."

Kirk found it pleasing that after giving them so much trouble the Aleph was, at long last, going to help them. He said, "While you're at it, you might study the inner workings of his augmented tractor beam generator and his Aleph generator. And see if you can discover why we couldn't beam him over here when we tried before."

"Aye, Captain. Such an investigation would surely give us the clues we need to counter Omen's tractor beam and his Alephs. As for the transporter, that may be a more complicated matter."

"More complicated than the Aleph?" Kirk asked with surprise.

"I fear so. The Aleph is really only a complex twist in the space-time continuum. On the other hand, a transporter beam is composed of a great many parts all working together. Using the Aleph, I may discover what wave cluster he blocked, or what combination of clusters, and we may be able to modify our beam accordingly. However, the modified beam may no longer be safe to use. We may beam him to the *Enterprise* only to discover that in the process we have seriously distorted his body or even killed him."

"I see. Then we will have to think of some other way to lure him over here."

Spock nodded and looked into his sensor scanner.

"Uhura, call Commodore Favere at Starbase 12 and advise him of our status. Ask him to send as many starships as he can round up. I don't want to deal with Omen alone."

"Aye, sir."

A few minutes later Uhura said, "Captain, I have Commodore Favere. He wishes to speak with you."

"On screen, Lieutenant."

When Favere's image came up, he said, "How is Ms. Payton?"

Kirk had been so preoccupied with catching Omen that he'd assumed Favere would want to talk about Starfleet matters. But he decided that Favere's question should not have surprised him. Kirk had been in love more than once, and he knew how the feeling could consume a person. He wondered, then, how honest he could be without unnecessarily frightening Favere. He decided that Favere would not thank him for watering down the news. "She's in sickbay. She had a rough time, but our Dr. McCoy says that all she needs is rest."

"What happened?"

"That's a very long story, Commodore. I'm sure Ms. Payton will want to regale you with it herself. Meanwhile, we need those ships."

Favere's jaw tightened, and his lips worked in and out. Kirk knew he wanted to know every detail of Payton's adventure.

Kirk said, "Trust me, Commodore, she's fine."

Favere apparently made a decision. He nodded and said, "The nearest ships will take some days to arrive at your present position. I gather you will not be there for long?"

If Kirk admitted the *Enterprise* was hunting for Professor Omen, he would have a lot of explaining to do, and Kirk didn't feel like explaining at the moment. He didn't have the time. He said, "We know the source of the starship disappearances, and we are going to stop it."

"You sound certain."

"I am."

"I see. Well, good hunting. And bring Ms. Payton back to me."

"That will be my pleasure."

Kirk's final statement was not entirely the truth. He continued to wonder what might have happened between himself and Payton if Favere had not been around. It was an idle speculation, and in some ways more romantic than the reality, because Kirk knew that the relationship would never be tested.

A few minutes later McCoy brought Payton onto the bridge. She was pale and hollow-eyed and frequently put her hand out for support, on the railing, on a chair, on McCoy. She looked and acted like a woman who had been through a long illness but was perhaps on the mend at last. She said that she was feeling better but did not wish to look into an Aleph ever again. With the air of someone changing the subject Payton asked Kirk, "How is Spock?"

"Stubborn, as usual," McCoy said. "If he doesn't get some rest soon, he's going to fall over in his traces."

Spock looked up from his viewer and, ignoring McCoy entirely, said, "I have *Erehwon's* present position, course, and speed."

"How long to reach it?" Kirk asked.

"At warp six we will arrive in eight hours, twenty minutes, forty-seven seconds."

"Will that give you enough time to modify our deflectors and phasers?"

"With the help of Mr. Scott and his staff, I believe so. The modifications are relatively simple, involving as they do the mathematics of only one universe."

"Very good," Kirk said. "Mr. Sulu, get your navigational data from Mr. Spock and engage warp engines immediately. Warp six."

"Aye, sir."

Kirk saw that Spock had not yet left the bridge. Spock claimed that he had succeeded in suppressing all his emotions, but still he had a body language—the hands behind his back, the height of his eyebrows, a thousand things Kirk had not consciously cataloged —that told him that Spock had more to say. Kirk said, "Something keeping you from engineering, Spock?"

"Yes, Captain. I believe you have another decision to make."

Kirk had no idea what that might be. It seemed to him that until they caught up with Omen the situation was covered. He said, "Decision-making is my job. What did I miss?"

Spock stepped down and stood at Kirk's right hand. "The Aleph. A ship that goes through an Aleph pulls it into the universe where the ship finds itself. That is why we haven't found an Aleph at every point where a ship disappeared."

"Understood, Spock. But that seems to be a purely technical matter."

"As you say, Captain. But the fact means that on our return we pulled an Aleph into this universe."

McCoy said, "Is there a point here, Spock, besides at the tip of each of your ears?"

Suddenly Kirk saw the end of Spock's line of reasoning, and it dismayed him. He said, "The Aleph is not just a weapon, Bones. It is also the ultimate spy apparatus. Whoever has one can, with the proper equipment and training, see anything."

"Indeed," said Spock. "However, the argument does have another side. The Aleph is an extraordinary topological construction representing a unique scientific achievement. It deserves study not by one person, or even by two, but by a team of scientists and mathematicians."

"Forget science for a moment, Spock," McCoy said. "Think of how your life would change if Starfleet could look over your shoulder any time without your knowing it."

"I have nothing to hide, Doctor."

McCoy leaned across Kirk and said, "Come now, Spock. We all have our little secrets. Vulcan secrets. Emotional secrets. Hmm?"

Spock considered that for a moment and then said, "I find your argument oddly compelling, Doctor."

Kirk said, "Are we talking about the Aleph out there? I thought you said it was unstable."

"So it seems from the mathematics, and I thought it best to move quickly lest I be correct. But no one can instantly grasp all the peculiarities of an object such as an Aleph. Frankly, I did not expect the Aleph to remain intact as long as it has. My question remains —do we destroy it or not?"

"What about Professor Omen's machine?" McCoy asked.

Payton asked, "What about Professor Omen himself? He could be looking in on us right now. After all, he has unlimited access to Alephs."

"Unlimited access, yes," said McCoy, "but he is a single-minded man. My guess is that as far as he's concerned, the Aleph is just a weapon."

"Dr. McCoy's suspicion would help explain why he was not here to meet us when we returned to this universe."

Kirk asked, "Can we destroy Omen's machine, Spock?"

Spock waited a moment, and then he chose his words carefully. He said, "It can be easily, uh, adjusted."

Kirk saw that he had a big decision to make, not only for the *Enterprise,* but for the Federation and perhaps for the entire galaxy. Once Professor Omen's Aleph technology became known, the secret of making Alephs would undoubtedly spread, and soon privacy would be a thing of the past. The Federation generally kept out of the private lives of its citizens, but how long could those in power withstand the temptation of taking just one peek? And would not one peek lead to a second?

And would the Klingons and the Romulans bother to ask such ethical questions? Would the Federation's own criminal element?

Once introduced into the body of Federation science, Kirk didn't think the Aleph could be withdrawn. If they destroyed this Aleph and "adjusted" the professor's machine, the universe would continue much as it did presently.

Kirk said, "Just because we *can* do something doesn't mean that we *should* do it."

"Agreed, Captain," Spock said. "But modifying the phasers will take several hours. Do you wish to give up that time to destroying this Aleph?"

"You can't do it long distance?" Kirk asked.

"No, sir. We must be in range of the phasers."

"Of course." Which was more important, catching up with Omen before he sent another starship to its death, or destroying this one Aleph which might soon expire on its own? Kirk said, "We'll postpone that decision for now. Uhura, drop a marker buoy within a thousand kilometers of the Aleph. Have it broadcast a wide-band signal warning away all ships."

"Aye, sir."

"Get down to engineering, Spock."

There were eight hours and change during which not much would be happening on the bridge. Kirk went to his cabin for a nap, and he fell asleep wondering what he would do with Omen when the *Enterprise* caught up with him. If beaming him aboard the *Enterprise* was out of the question, Kirk could see only one other alternative. He hoped it was clever enough.

He awoke and went over the plan in his mind. He ran through it again in the shower, and then went to the rec room on Deck 6, where he ordered the replicator to make him a roast beef sandwich, salad, and coffee. He turned around with his tray in his hands and saw Payton sitting by herself at the end of a table. She was taking slow sips from a steaming cup. He walked over to her and asked if he could sit down.

She smiled at him drowsily and said, "Of course."

Kirk sat down and began to gnaw on the ragged edges of beef around the outside of the bread. They ate in companionable silence for a while, and then Kirk said, "One of the few things that Spock and McCoy agree on is that if you hadn't been here, the *Enterprise* would have been stuck forever in that empty pocket-universe."

"That's nice of them, but I think they give me too much credit."

"I don't think so. Our sensors were shot. The only

effective method we had for looking into the Aleph was through your implant."

"Credit the implant then."

"And credit your cooperation," Kirk said.

She smiled. "And my cooperation. From Hazel Payton, the woman who gets the job done."

"Thank goodness," Kirk said. He liked this woman a lot, and he could not help wondering again what might have happened if Favere had not been in the picture. He said, "Not many have studied the Aleph."

"No. We have that in common." The thought that they had things in common momentarily saddened Payton. Without looking at Kirk, she said, "I don't remember much of what I saw. More of it fades all the time."

Kirk realized that she was right. The whole Aleph experience seemed more and more like a dream. He said, "I guess we have some surprises left to us after all."

Payton nodded as she glanced around. Then she peered at Kirk and said seriously, "But you and your senior officers are much too modest. If they hadn't known the capabilities of the *Enterprise* so well, if they hadn't been so creative and highly skilled, we'd still be in the pocket universe, implant or not."

"I thought Starfleet was interested only in war and conquest." Kirk opened his sandwich and began to pick out shreds of meat and put them in his mouth.

"I guess," said Payton, "we both learned something on this voyage."

"Another *Enterprise* miracle," Kirk said, chuckling. He felt extraordinarily good. Whatever happened, it was a pleasure to be sitting there with Payton. The fact that he was delivering her to another man did not change that.

"Not just a miracle," Payton said. "I found out that *Enterprise* has an ethical man in command."

Kirk was gratified, of course, but also surprised Payton had thought to tell him this. "How do you figure that?"

"I've had a chance to watch you with your crew. These people like you and respect you. That sort of balance is not easy to achieve. And then there's the matter of the Klingee Association." She grinned at him.

"Oh?"

"Yes. You could have blown them away with that first phaser blast, but you chose not to. You chose to talk your way out of the situation."

"They had the cyclor."

"You didn't know that till they hit you with it."

"I guess not."

Kirk picked at his sandwich, and Payton drank her tea. Crew members moved around them but kept their distance. Soon Kirk would have to return to the bridge and face Omen. Defeating him would be a challenge, but he welcomed it. That's why he'd joined Starfleet, why he was out there: he liked to test himself against challenges that no one had met before.

When he was done eating Kirk left Payton, still nursing that same cup of tea, and went down to engineering. "How's it coming?" he asked.

"Our work is nearly completed," said Spock.

"Aye," said Scott. "What a patchwork you've made of my poor ship." He shook his head.

"It's for a good cause, Mr. Scott," Kirk assured him. "You're sure Omen's augmented tractor beam will not be able to get a grip on our deflectors?"

"That is our goal, Captain."

"And our phasers will be able to destroy Alephs?"

"So it would seem."

Damn Spock. Sometimes he could be so noncommittal, his answers were less informative than no answers at all. Brusquely Kirk asked, "You've tested them?"

"As far as possible."

"Aye," said Scott. "Only computer simulations, but fairly reliable for all that."

Kirk nodded and said, "According to Spock, attempting to beam Omen over here would be dangerous."

"Not to us," Scott said. The thought that the attempt might be dangerous to Omen did not seem to bother him.

"I'll need tractor beams to haul *Erehwon* back to Starbase 12."

"Aye, we can do it," said Scott. "But we might have better luck if we used an augmented tractor beam of our own."

"Can we do that?" Kirk asked.

Spock said, "Omen's tractor beam is based on the same technical innovation that produced his new deflectors. The beam is phased, switching on and off thousands of times every nanosecond. It is, in fact, this phasing that will allow us to escape his grip."

"I can have an augmented tractor beam on line in a few minutes," Scotty assured Kirk.

"And have Omen slip away from us as easily as we

can slip away from him? I don't think so. Give *Enterprise*'s normal tractor beam maximum power. If that doesn't work, we'll try something else."

For a moment Spock and Scott considered Kirk's idea. Scott said, "Aye. Sometimes it's smarter to fight fire with water than with fire."

Spock said, "I would not have explained my position in such a colorful manner, Mr. Scott, but essentially you state the case correctly."

The bosun's whistle came on the air, and Uhura called over the intercom, "Bridge to Captain Kirk."

Kirk punched the intercom switch and asked what was wanted.

"We have *Erehwon* in sensor range."

"Thank you, Lieutenant. Mr. Spock and I will be right up." Kirk turned to Scott and said, "I'll want those phasers and tractor beams on demand."

"You'll have them, sir."

On the turbolift Kirk had some time to consider the challenge that awaited him when he reached the bridge. He was up against a genius equipped with weapons a full step ahead of any aboard the *Enterprise*. Weapons on the *Enterprise* were jury-rigged to make up the difference, but Scotty's comment about a patchwork was more accurate than Kirk liked.

When Kirk and Spock arrived on the bridge Uhura said, "We're being hailed by *Erehwon,* Captain. Evidently Omen saw us at about the same time we saw him."

With a sigh Kirk settled into his command chair and allowed himself a moment to contemplate the stars on the screen. It was a big universe, and evidently an infinite number of universes resembled it to some degree. In how many of them was a starship like his about to meet an asteroid like *Erehwon?* In how many of them would the starship triumph? Kirk said, "On screen, Lieutenant."

The face of Omen appeared on screen. He made such a pretense of not being impressed by what anybody else did, Kirk found gauging his attitude difficult. Still, there were indicators: Omen's jaw was set, and a muscle ticked below his right eye. Kirk said, "Surprised to see us, Professor?"

"How did you do it, Captain? How did you escape from the Aleph?" He had all the attributes of a thirsty man demanding to know the location of water.

Behind Kirk Spock spoke in low tones. *"Erehwon* approaching, sir. Estimated time of arrival three minutes, forty-two seconds."

"Shields, Mr. Chekov."

"Aye, Captain."

Apparently Kirk's trap was working. "You're not the only one who can do impossible things before breakfast," Kirk said. "I'm sure Mr. Spock and Mr. Scott would be pleased to show you the mathematics."

"Bother the mathematics," Omen said. "How did you find your way back here?"

"It's not a secret. Return with us to Starbase 12, and we'll tell you everything."

Every part of Omen's face moved independently. With an act of great will Omen got himself under control. Still, curiosity worked strongly in him. His need to know what had happened must have been almost physical in its intensity.

The ship shook, and its hull rang as if a god had struck it with a hammer.

"View forward," Kirk said.

Omen was replaced by stars, now stationary. A light grew among them—*Erehwon.*

Spock said, *"Erehwon's* augmented tractor beam is holding the *Enterprise,* Captain."

"Mr. Sulu, reverse one quarter impulse."

"One quarter impulse, aye."

The impulse engines strained.

"We're moving, sir," Chekov said.

"That should irritate him," Kirk said to himself. More loudly, he said, "All stop, Mr. Sulu. Mr. Spock, prepare tractor beam."

Immediately Spock said, "Ready, sir."

"Take *Erehwon* in tow and proceed at one half impulse."

The impulse engines began to grind again. Chekov said, "Captain, we're not moving."

"Spock?" Kirk demanded.

"We are securely joined, Captain. But I believe that Omen has once again employed his hyper-anchor."

"Give me a channel," Kirk said.

"Open, sir."

"Omen, this won't do you any good. Most of Starfleet will be here soon. You can't make Alephs fast enough to trap us all." Would "soon" be soon enough? Kirk wondered. Favere had said it would be days before the first ships arrived. Could he and Omen keep each other at bay for days?

"Captain," Spock called. "Sensors picking up a ship—closing fast."

Kirk whirled in his chair. "Already? Favere said—"

"Not Federation, sir," Spock said. "Klingon."

Real Klingons, Kirk knew. Klingons who would not be impressed by a simple trick like the one that had routed the Klingees.

Chapter Fourteen

ENTERPRISE AND *EREHWON* were locked together with their hands at each other's throats. On the main screen, near *Erehwon,* the Klingon ship waited like a vulture, ready to pick the bones of the loser. Kirk could not decide whether the distraction of the Klingons' arrival benefited him, Omen, or neither.

"We're being hailed by the Klingon vessel, sir."

"On screen, Lieutenant."

"A moment, Captain," Spock said. "Maintaining a hold on *Erehwon* is putting considerable stress on the ship. Power levels are down ten percent and dropping. Our tractor beam was not designed for this kind of use."

Kirk did not like mistreating his ship this way, but if he let *Erehwon* go, it would destroy more ships before anyone could find it again. *If* they could find it again.

Omen was a clever man. He would adapt. "Hang on, Spock, and please advise Mr. Scott to do the same. Uhura, put the Klingons on screen."

The disheartening tableau of *Erehwon* and the Klingon ship was replaced by the face of an angry Klingon. Even if he hadn't known what universe he was in, Kirk would have been certain that this was no Klingee.

"Torm," Kirk said with surprise. This was the same Klingon who'd accused him of disintegrating the Empire's ships. After all they'd been through, what a joke that seemed.

Torm sneered when he said, "Now I know why my science officer could not identify the energy fluctuations emanating from these coordinates. We've found your secret Starfleet weapon!"

How could Kirk convince the Klingon he was wrong about the Aleph? Desperately Kirk said, "Torm, wait. It's not a Federation weapon." Kirk sounded ridiculous, even in his own ears. Torm had no reason to believe him. And yet what could Kirk do? *Enterprise* could not join in a firefight with *Kormak* without letting go of *Erehwon*. In which case *Erehwon* would certainly escape while the *Enterprise* and the *Kormak* were busy taking shots at each other, thus making their fight pointless. If only the Klingon would listen!

Torm looked ready to spit. He said, "I expected you to claim as much."

"It's not a Starfleet weapon, but otherwise you're right. This *is* the source of the disappearances. We've found it, and the man running the operation is under arrest." It would do no harm for Kirk to admit this. If he was half as bright as advertised, Omen had already guessed what Kirk had in mind.

"Federation arrest. A lot of talk, then three months of coddling. I will do your job for you, Kirk. End transmission."

"Torm!" Kirk cried.

Seconds later the hot blue tongue of a disrupter beam licked out from the *Kormak* and swept the space around the *Erehwon*. The disrupter beam wasn't able to touch the asteroid, repelled as it was by Omen's new shields. The shields glowed softly, hardly bothered by the Klingon attack.

After a moment Torm stopped wasting energy.

Kirk was frustrated. He could join *Kormak* in its attack on *Erehwon*. He could attack the *Kormak* in an attempt to save the *Erehwon*, though at the moment the *Erehwon* didn't appear to need saving. Neither of these plans appealed to Kirk.

Perhaps the best course of action was to do nothing at all. Allow *Kormak* to attack *Erehwon* until Torm became discouraged. At that point it was likely *Kormak* would attack the *Enterprise*. But that did not bother Kirk. He knew how to fight Klingons. Payton might get her battle footage after all.

Of course, to save the *Enterprise* Kirk would have to allow the *Erehwon* to escape; but given that kind of alternative, only one choice was possible.

Suddenly a spinning diamond bloomed on the side of the *Erehwon* and rushed toward *Kormak*. It was an Aleph. Torm fired at it, to no effect, and Kirk cried, "Fire phasers at the Aleph now, Mr. Sulu."

Sulu was acting even as he said, "Aye, sir."

The phaser touched the Aleph, and the Aleph

shattered, tearing itself apart like an unbalanced wheel. The shards flew away, turning, showing scenes, objects, people, eventually fading, the shards smoothing themselves back into the fabric of the universe.

"We're being hailed by the *Kormak*," Uhura said.

"What a surprise," Sulu said.

"On screen."

"What was that?" Torm demanded.

"That was an Aleph," Kirk said. "It is the weapon you're looking for." Let Torm believe the Aleph was a disintegrator of some kind. Kirk saw no reason to explain what the Aleph really did.

"We did not ask for your help. By saving us," Torm said, "you insult our reputation as warriors."

The famous Klingon pride. You couldn't even do them a favor without their taking offense. Kirk shrugged and smiled in a way he hoped would show he was trying to be reasonable. He opened his hands and said, "Let's just say you owe us one."

Torm was about to give some retort when Kirk added impulsively, "You might tell us about the cyclor, for instance."

Torm's eyes opened wide, and his jaw dropped. His skin darkened. Kirk had never seen a Klingon look so surprised. "How did you . . ."

The channel went dead, and they were looking at *Erehwon* and *Kormak* again.

"What happened, Lieutenant?"

"*Kormak* ended transmission, sir."

Kirk chuckled and said, "If you can't convince them, confuse them, eh, Spock?"

Spock said, "You would have confused them more had they not heard of a cyclor."

The Klingee and the Klingons had their obvious differences, but they seemed to have similar technologies. If the Klingons did not have the cyclor now, they would probably have it soon. Kirk said, "It was a good bet."

Spock raised an eyebrow but said nothing.

Uhura said, "Sir, the *Kormak* is sending a coded subspace message."

"I don't have to know the code to guess Torm is informing the Empire that we know about the cyclor."

"Undoubtedly," Spock said.

"How's our tractor beam doing?"

"Holding, Captain. So far."

"That's all I ask. Hail Omen, Lieutenant."

"Aye, sir." A moment later Uhura said, "No answer, sir."

Was Omen sulking or preparing a surprise for them? Omen was a genius, and it would not do to underestimate him. Kirk said, "I'll assume he's listening. I'd be listening if I were him. Broadcast on the frequency we've been using."

"Aye, sir."

Spock said, "The Klingons are certainly listening, too."

"I'm counting on it."

Kirk raised his voice and said, "Professor Omen, this is Captain Kirk. I'd advise you to surrender. If Starfleet doesn't get you, the Klingons certainly will, and with less concern for your welfare."

Kirk waited, and what he'd hoped for happened. Torm entered the conversation growling. He said, "Kirk is correct. Your shields are effective, but we will discover their secret and carve you like a *p'tach!*" He pronounced the Klingon word as if he were clearing his throat.

Still nothing from *Erehwon*.

Kirk said, "Listen to me, Professor. We have data on your new deflectors, on your augmented tractor beam, and even on your Aleph. You are not the only weapons expert in the galaxy. Trust me: You cannot keep a step ahead of the Federation forever. Or of the Klingons. Not forever. Not even you."

Still nothing from *Erehwon*. Omen was leaving Kirk no choice. He would have to destroy the asteroid if he could, though he did not want to. Kirk knew that Omen had the right idea. Peace was the way. But Kirk didn't think that peace could be imposed by anyone, no matter the intentions, no matter the level of technology. And how long would peace stick, even if Omen succeeded? Until one being wanted something another being had. In the minds of many, sweet reason would never replace a quick jab to the chops.

This pessimism disturbed Kirk. As a military man his goal had always been to put himself out of business. But a deep, realistic part of himself didn't think this was possible, any more than it was possible for McCoy to put himself out of business, whatever McCoy's wishes.

"Can we hold him till the fleet gets here?" Kirk asked, though he knew the answer.

"We can hold him for another two hours fourteen minutes," Spock said. "After that, maintaining hull integrity will be increasingly difficult."

"Omen," Kirk cried. "Are you listening to me? There are other ways to work for peace."

Suddenly Omen appeared on the screen. He looked

as if he hadn't slept in days, but more than that, Kirk judged his soul to be weary, as if he'd been fighting his own nature. That was the basic weakness in ethical men: Even when they were certain they were right, they still doubted themselves. A bit of them was never convinced. And that caused them to lose sleep and appetite.

"I hear you, Captain," Omen said, "and I believe you are correct. The galaxy is full of weapons experts, and sooner or later they will discover my secrets. You already have the new deflectors, and perhaps the augmented tractor beam as well. They are trifles compared to what I have in mind. And it is my mind that you want. If you take *Erehwon* intact, you will study the plans and prototypes aboard. If you take me alive, you will force me to make weapons of war again."

Kirk wondered if that was true. Would the Federation force him to build weapons? Kirk said, "Professor, I—"

Omen went on as if Kirk had not spoken. "I cannot allow either of these things to occur. For the sake of my daughter. For the sake of all the children. Goodbye, Captain. Perhaps we will meet again in a better universe."

The screen returned to the scene outside. With a sudden fearful knowledge of imminent disaster Kirk leapt for Spock's control board and pressed one of the keys. As if a tug-of-war rope had been suddenly cut, *Enterprise* flew backwards, away from the Aleph that now spun where *Erehwon* had been. Everyone was thrown forward while the inertial compensators tried to make up for the sudden movement. When he looked up Kirk saw that the Aleph was gone, too, sucked into whatever universe *Erehwon* now inhabited.

"Impulse power to compensate," Kirk said.

"Aye," Sulu said as he applied braking power.

"Hail the *Kormak*," Kirk said, though he had no interest in speaking with the Klingons. He was tired. He'd just provoked a good man to commit suicide as surely as if Omen had had a painful and fatal wasting disease and Kirk had been the first to tell him about it. It was possible that Omen had gone to a universe where he could live and perhaps even be happy. But Kirk's universe would never see him again. Omen was shut behind the wall of the Aleph as surely as a dead person was shut behind the impenetrable wall that separated life from death.

Torm appeared on the screen, a crafty expression on his face. Kirk tried to imagine what Torm must be thinking. He did not trust Kirk or anyone of the Federation. Yet it must seem to him that Kirk had just solved one of the Empire's problems. Was it a trick? Had the entire drama been played out strictly for the Empire's benefit? Torm said, "What happened?"

"You had a free home demonstration of the weapon."

"This Earther, this Omen, as you call him, destroyed himself to prevent us from capturing him?"

In its simplest form he supposed that Torm was right, and Kirk admitted as much.

Torm nodded and said, "He was a worthy adversary. But what of the weapon?"

"What of it?"

"You were able to destroy the spinning fireball. Perhaps you are also able to make one."

Spock could probably make an Aleph generator, but he would not. Not everything that could be made should be made.

Kirk said, "The secret died with Omen."

"We shall see," Torm said. He was about to ask something else, perhaps how Kirk knew about the cyclor. Instead he saluted Kirk in the Klingon manner and ended the transmission.

"Power configuration of *Kormak* is changing."

For a moment Kirk thought that Torm meant to attack them, but the Klingon ship turned and shot away. It was soon no more than a moving star among stars, and then even that was gone.

"His course is for the Klingon Empire, Captain."

"Good news at last," Kirk said. "Mr. Chekov, set a course for Starbase 12."

Chekov consulted the astrogation display, inputted his coordinates, and said, "Course laid in. Twelve hours at warp four."

Kirk thought of Payton and Favere and said, "Warp six, Mr. Sulu. Engage."

That evening after his watch, after dinner, Spock went to his cabin—to meditate, he said. Kirk hoped it would be as satisfying to him as a well-deserved nap would be to a human. Kirk had eaten with him, but conversation had been sparse. Sometimes it was like that after a mission. Everything had been said, and they would not think of new things to say till time insulated them from their most recent trials.

Kirk went to the observation lounge on Deck 10 of the ship's dorsal. He looked out at the rainbow smudges that passed for stars in warp space. The smudges closed behind them, as if *Enterprise* were a burrowing animal, grabbing the medium of warp space in front and flinging it back to fill behind. Kirk knew this was all romance, of course. The mathematics of the warp drive mentioned no burrowing, no flinging. And yet the illusion was, in its way, very convincing and not without its comfort. For when she was a billion kilometers from anywhere the notion that the *Enterprise* was an animal with some concern for her symbiotic crew was as comforting as it was ridiculous.

He became aware of the air blowers, and of the unusual mix of odors—plastic, metal, cleaning compounds, fabric, alien bodies, cooled and recycled air—that made a starship smell the way it did.

For many hours he'd been thinking about Omen and his weapons of peace. He'd learned that second-guessing himself was always a frustrating business, even after he reminded himself that being a starship captain should be a learning experience. This time Kirk could see nothing that he'd done wrong, nothing that he would have done differently, nothing that would have ended in saving Omen. Everything had seemed like a good idea at the time. That was all he could ask of himself. All anyone could ask.

As was sometimes the case, the safety of the ship had come down to depending on the swift action of one man. It was not always so, but in this case it was the action of the captain that had counted. His job was to throw one switch, to disconnect the tractor beam and thereby prevent the ship from being sucked with *Erehwon* into the Aleph.

Kirk let his mind run free. War, peace, and *Erehwon* circled like fish in the aquarium of his head.

"Excuse me, Captain," McCoy said.

Kirk turned and saw him and Payton standing at the door to the lounge, uncertain whether they should enter.

"Come in, Bones, Ms. Payton. I've been alone with my own thoughts long enough."

McCoy said, "And Spock?"

"Meditating."

"Ah," said McCoy, as if that one word explained everything.

"How are you feeling, Ms. Payton?" Kirk asked.

"Much better, thank you, though I can't seem to convince the doctor of that." She smiled as she spoke, taking the sting out of the words.

"Oh, I'm convinced," McCoy said. "But where is it written that a doctor can't take an after-dinner stroll with his patient?"

They watched the rainbow smudges for a long time. Then Payton said, "I'm really sorry, Captain. I feel as if I committed treason or something."

"Treason?" asked Kirk. It was a new idea.

"Yes. Mr. Kent and I were colluding with the man who was destroying ships. Because of us, the *Enterprise* almost vanished forever."

McCoy was about to say something, but instead he waited and looked expectantly at Kirk.

Payton's question made Kirk uneasy. He liked her and had even succeeded in convincing himself that Conrad Franklin Kent was wrong but sincere. Treason against the Federation was a crime so heinous he could barely comprehend that someone he liked would consider herself capable of it. He said, "I don't think so."

Kirk's statement opened the floodgates of McCoy's impassioned opinion. "Of course not, my dear," he said. He went on to argue that neither Payton nor Kent had known exactly what Omen had in mind when he offered to prove that Starfleet was more interested in war than in exploration—Omen had admitted that himself—and therefore neither of them could be held accountable. He went on, piling argument on top of argument, as if Payton herself were a judge who had to be convinced.

At the start of McCoy's speech Payton seemed mystified, but as he went on she brightened up, and by the end of it she was laughing at McCoy's overwhelming enthusiasm and increasingly outrageous hyperbole. At last she was pleased to agree that McCoy was right.

"I told you I didn't think so," Kirk said, and they all shared a laugh. A moment later he said, "Now I have a question for *you*."

Payton made an interrogative noise.

"You originally came on board to write a report for Conrad Franklin Kent. Is that still your intention?"

Very seriously Payton said, "Yes, it is."

"I see." Kirk looked at the floor. As far as he could tell, very little had happened on this voyage that Kent could use as ammunition in his crusade against Starfleet. But he also had enough experience with diplomacy to know that facts could be manipulated. In this respect he imagined that politics and show business were not much different—from each other or from diplomacy. If Kent wanted to knock Starfleet, he would do it with the materials at hand, no matter what they were.

Payton said, "I am, after all, a woman who gets the job done."

Kirk and McCoy nodded.

"It's just too bad that Mr. Kent will certainly not approve of my report."

They looked at her with surprise. "He'll fire you," McCoy said.

"Maybe. But I've known Mr. Kent for a few years, and I think that something else will actually happen. I think he'll read my report, see the error of his ways, and change his mind about Starfleet."

As much as Kirk liked Payton—or maybe *because* he liked her so much—he was able to see the other side, her side. For this reason also he was still not convinced that she would put together a positive report from her implant recordings. Self-preservation might become a higher priority than saving Starfleet, and if it did, he could not fault her. Why be loyal to Starfleet, just another branch of government, a branch that should be sawed away if it was rotten? And he was even less confident about Kent's flexibility.

Kirk said, "That would be a pleasant surprise."

McCoy said, "If he does change his mind, I might even support him."

Kirk grunted. He did not care to comment on McCoy's statement. Who a man supported for president was a citizen's private business. But, Kirk thought, there was such a thing as going too far to make a point.

Chapter Fifteen

As ENTERPRISE APPROACHED STARBASE 12 messages flashed between them. Some came from Commodore Favere and were official. After asking whether the mission had been a success Favere asked about the safety of crew and passengers. Kirk knew Favere's question was a thinly veiled plea to know if Hazel Payton was all right, and Kirk obliged him by reporting that she was.

When Favere asked about Omen Kirk hesitated for a moment before he said, "He is no longer with us."

"You mean he's dead?" Favere asked, astonished.

"Not dead," said Kirk. He did not want to be evasive, yet he felt the fact of Omen's final destination was less important than the understanding of the incidents that had forced Omen to take such drastic action. Any answer, Kirk knew, was bound to be incomplete and unsatisfying and would only lead to more questions. Kirk said, "Commodore, you can do us both a favor and wait for my official report."

"If you wish," Favere said a little stiffly.

Other messages were from Conrad Franklin Kent and, though not official, asked many of the same questions. Kirk was less inclined to answer them. He did say, "I think you'll find Ms. Payton's report to be unlike anything you had in mind."

Kent chuckled down in his warm inside cupboards and said, "I think you're wrong, Captain. Ms. Payton is not a likely candidate for brainwashing."

"Mr. Kent, I assure you that brainwashing was never an option."

"Let me speak with her."

"You can talk to her all you want on Starbase 12." In Kirk's mind his present conversation was haunted by the ghost of an earlier conversation in which Kent had refused to answer questions, saying only that Professor Omen would tell Kirk everything he wanted to know. Turnabout was fair play, as far as Kirk was concerned.

When he found that Kirk would not part with any more information Kent angrily broke the connection. This gave Kirk a certain amount of satisfaction, for which he could not bring himself to feel guilty.

As *Enterprise* navigated close to Starbase 12 Spock pointed out the sorry condition of the class-J freighter that had been the object of the deflector test.

"Are you sure that's the same freighter?" Kirk asked with surprise. It seemed unlikely. When last seen the freighter had been dented from its years of service, but undamaged by everything *Enterprise* could throw at her. The freighter they were passing looked as if she had encountered a cloud of acid. Large jagged holes yearned toward one another as if the hull were made of paper and had been touched here and there with a lighted match. Most of the tail section was gone, leaving only the framework of the vertical stabilizer, a basket in which to catch nothing. Deep in the hulk short-circuits occasionally sparked, briefly lighting corridors and machinery, casting shadows that took little imagination to make into massive and ill-proportioned monsters.

"I remember the serial number clearly, Captain," Spock said.

"I'm sure you do, Mr. Spock. But if that's the case, what happened?"

"What indeed?"

A few minutes later Kirk, Spock, and McCoy stood in the transporter room waiting for Ms. Payton. Spock was idly watching Mr. Kyle check settings on the transporter control board. McCoy had assured Kirk that Payton could do nothing but write a favorable report and now was going on about his intentions toward a buffalo steak smothered in mushrooms and onions. "Why can't Scotty program our replicators for that kind of food?"

"I'll speak to him about it," Kirk said. He was in total agreement about the steak, but other, less certain matters crowded his mind. The condition of the freighter was only one of the things Kirk was considering.

He was not worried, precisely, but he could not help wondering what Payton had finally written in her report; she had refused even to discuss the matter except to say that she was working on it. Kirk felt McCoy was something of a romantic in his view that Payton was certain to write a favorable report.

Admiral Nogura would certainly not be pleased that Kirk was responsible for the virtual suicide of one of the Federation's leading scientists. Nogura could be made to understand, of course. He was not an unreasonable man. After he understood, Nogura would probably give the crew of the *Enterprise* medals. But Kirk did not look forward to the intensive examination that was sure to come before understanding occurred.

The doors slid open, and Payton entered carrying a small gray duffel bag from one shoulder. And something was missing from her hair—the implant. If Payton felt recording everything was no longer necessary, then the mission really was over.

Mostly for Payton's benefit, Kirk asked, "Everybody ready?"

Nods all around. They climbed onto the transporter stage, and Mr. Kyle energized. The transporter room broke up like a bad signal, to be replaced by the transporter room of Starbase 12. They might still have been aboard the *Enterprise* but for the Amerind ceremonial drums on the back wall, the absence of Mr. Kyle, and the presence of Mr. Kent and Commodore Favere.

Kirk nodded at Kent and said it was good to see Favere again. He handed Favere the gold wafer on which a copy of the ship's log was recorded and said, "I think this will answer all your questions. If it doesn't, you might try reading the report Ms. Payton has prepared." He could not prevent an edge of sarcasm from sharpening his voice.

"I will keep that in mind."

Favere watched with hungry anticipation while Payton greeted Kent and handed him the blue wafer that held her report. She said, "I think you'll find it interesting."

Kent nodded and smiled. He did not wink knowingly, which disappointed Kirk a little. It seemed to him to be a lost opportunity. Kent said, "I hope this explains what happened to Professor Omen."

"It does," Payton said.

She went to Favere and took both his hands. The public familiarity seemed to astonish him, but happily so. The formal manner in which he proceeded to welcome her to Starbase 12 made McCoy smile. Kirk smiled, too, despite his feeling a little jealousy at Favere's good fortune. Timing, Kirk decided again, was everything. Kent frowned but said nothing. Spock merely seemed content to watch the scene play itself out.

Payton said, "I want to make this announcement in front of the people who are closest to me."

Payton shocked Kirk. He tried to remember if he'd ever heard her speak of family on Earth or anywhere else in the Federation. He couldn't remember one way or the other.

She looked Favere in the eye and went on as if no one else was there, "Before we went out on this mission you asked me to marry you. I had some problems with that and gave you an evasive answer. But in the last week or so I had occasion, more than once to believe I would never see you again, and the thought hurt me so much I could barely stand it. I learned my lesson. So if you're still interested, I am saying 'yes.'"

For a moment Favere appeared to be too astonished to reply. He stared at Payton wide-eyed and with his chin a little slack, then nodded as he slowly regained control. Offhandedly he said, "I guess you could say I'm still interested," and he grinned.

The tension was broken. Kirk, feeling very noble indeed, congratulated Favere and Payton. Kent forced himself to shake hands with Favere and managed to croak out a "Congratulations" in Payton's direction. McCoy insisted on kissing the bride, though he claimed the right to do it again at the wedding.

Kent said, "If you'll excuse me, I have a report to read." He rushed from the transporter room as if he were about to explode and did not want to do it there.

"Well," said Kirk, "I'm sure that Ms. Payton and the commodore have a lot to discuss."

Spock said, "Indeed. Commodore Favere will also want to read the ship's log."

"Of course," said Kirk. After living all these years among humans, Spock still missed some of the nuances. Or perhaps he only enjoyed playing the somber Vulcan even as McCoy enjoyed twitting him for it.

Kirk flipped open his communicator and told Uhura to start shore leave rotation. He was pleased to be giving his crew some time off at last. Hell, he was pleased to be getting it himself. Lacking another emergency call, *Enterprise* would be at Starbase 12 for at least a week.

Favere said, "Mr. Spock is right. Duty comes first.

We'll meet again with Mr. Kent in a few hours. I'm sure he'll have some comments to make."

"I love Starfleet," Payton said, and she punched Favere gently in the shoulder.

"Thank you, Commodore," Kirk said. He turned to Spock and McCoy. "Who's for Enyart's?"

Kirk, Spock, and McCoy settled in a dim alcove of the Starbase 12 Enyart's. Kirk ordered English beer, McCoy had a champagne cocktail (to celebrate surviving yet another trip on the transporter, he said), and Spock had tea. It was not Vulcan tea, but, with his customary stoicism, he made do. Shortly Kirk and McCoy were enjoying buffalo steaks smothered in mushrooms and onions. In the spirit of the occasion Spock agreed to have mushrooms and onions, but *only* mushrooms and onions.

Conversation centered around what Payton's report might say and how Kent might react to it. At first Spock refused to be drawn in, protesting that he didn't have enough data to make a determination. But McCoy goaded him a little, and at last Spock admitted that experience with his mother assured him he had no idea what an Earth woman might do in a given situation.

McCoy threw an arm across Spock's shoulder and said, "My pointy-eared friend, you are not alone."

A moment later McCoy asked, "What about your log, Jim?"

"What about it?" Kirk answered a little defensively. He knew what McCoy had in mind and had been thinking about it himself.

"Do you present Payton and Kent as traitors or not?"

"I present the facts, Bones. As always."

Spock said, "And yet the doctor poses an interesting question. Mr. Kent forced you to take Ms. Payton on board for a purpose other than the one stated."

Kirk's arguments were ready. He'd thought about them while preparing his logs for Commodore Favere. He said, "Ms. Payton never prevented us from searching for the weapon. It was the arrival of *Erehwon* that temporarily sidetracked us. And if we are to believe Ms. Payton, neither she nor Mr. Kent knew about the Aleph before we did. As far as they were concerned, Omen was just going to help them with their anti-Starfleet campaign."

Spock folded his arms and said, "I might add that if Ms. Payton and her implant had not been aboard, we would still be in the empty universe."

"I'm with you two," McCoy said expansively. "All Payton and Kent are guilty of is a little bad judgment. It's something we're all guilty of from time to time."

"True, Doctor," said Spock. "It is a common human failing."

"Vulcans never make bad decisions?" McCoy asked.

"They never make illogical decisions. Logic saves Vulcans from the worst of judgmental errors."

The conversation continued, with first McCoy and then Spock taking the upper hand. Kirk only half listened. He was thinking about Payton's report and the meeting to come.

Presently, in the way of such things, all they had before them were dirty plates. Coffee came for Kirk and McCoy. Spock had more tea. Around them crew members of the *Enterprise* ate and drank with their friends. Kirk and the others returned nods and greetings when they were offered.

At the sound of the bosun's whistle the noise level momentarily dropped to a muffled drone, and a voice said, "Captain Kirk and party are invited to the commodore's office at their earliest convenience. Repeating . . ."

While the voice repeated the message Kirk said, "Here we go."

On their way to Commodore Favere's office Kirk reflected that this would probably be a dress rehearsal for the meeting he was sure to have with Nogura. As such, he would take full advantage of it.

They were shown into Favere's office to find Payton and Kent already there. Payton and Favere tried not to be engrossed in each other, but they could not help sharing small smiles; their pleasure in being together was almost palpable. When not distracted by Payton Favere pushed around a small brass bullet on his desk. Kent's expression was neutral, unreadable. He knocked the blue wafer against one crossed ankle.

"Please sit down, Kirk," Favere said.

Kirk settled into the remaining empty chair. Spock and McCoy stood at their customary positions on either side. Before the main event began Kirk took the initiative and asked a question to which *he* wanted an answer. He cleared his throat.

"Yes, Kirk?"

"On the way in we passed the test freighter. What happened to it?"

"That's right," Favere said. "You left before we got the bad news." He took the bullet up in his fist as if to squeeze an answer out of it.

"Bad news?" Spock asked.

Favere explained, "Shortly after you left, the freighter began to fall apart. I am told the process is continuing even now." Responding to Spock's raised eyebrow, Favere went on. "While Omen's phased deflectors are effective against phasers and photon torpedoes, they also have an unpredicted side effect. The field changes the crystalline structure of metal, and the ship quickly disintegrates. Omen's first assistant, Bahia Slocum, is working on the problem, but"—Favere shrugged—"we were hoping Professor Omen could find a remedy for us." He dropped the bullet onto his desktop and pursed his lips at it for a moment, giving everyone a chance to consider Omen's sins and the fine mess those sins had gotten him into.

"If I can be of any service—" Spock began.

Favere said, "Thank you. I will inform Ms. Slocum of your offer."

It was odd, Kirk decided, how Omen's professional luck had turned. He had perfected the phaser and the photon torpedo, but his later work was not nearly so successful. The deflectors didn't work because they caused the ships they protected to fall apart. The augmented tractor beam didn't work because its very nature allowed its target to slip away. Only the Aleph worked, and ultimately it was the only one of his inventions that Omen *needed* to work. Perhaps it was just as well that Omen had absented himself. His recent failures would surely cause his reputation to suffer, and Omen would not have liked that. Despite science, despite logic, the universe remained unpredictable even for such men as Omen.

Even for the members of Starfleet. For a moment Kirk was impressed and a little frightened by how dangerous his job really was. The chill passed like a cold gust of wind, and all that remained of the feeling was the spice of danger, of new discovery, of challenge, the things for which he'd gone into space. With new confidence Kirk said, "Don't worry. Those phased deflectors probably wouldn't stand up against a cyclor anyway."

Kent frowned, and Favere appeared to be uncomfortable. Favere said, "Mr. Kent informs me that the Federation has known for some time that the Klingons were developing a cyclor. But the information is top secret."

Kirk shrugged. Lightly he said, "The existence of the cyclor is not the only secret my crew and I know, Commodore. I assume Mr. Kent trusts Ms. Payton?"

"I do," Kent said.

"Then your secret is safe. Commodore, you'll notice that my log has the most complete sensor report of which *Enterprise* was capable at the time of the cyclor attack. I suggest you turn it over to Bahia Slocum. In the absence of Professor Omen, she is the best person to analyze it."

"She's working on the deflector problem at the moment," Kent reminded him.

Kirk smiled and said, "It was only a suggestion." For the moment he was in control of the meeting. He asked the questions and had many of the answers. He wondered if he'd only beaten them to the punch, if either Kent or Favere would eventually have gotten around to asking him about the cyclor, or if they'd decided among themselves not to mention it in the hope that Kirk would not realize its importance and soon forget it. Their hope was vain as far as Kirk was concerned.

With a loud click Kent set the blue wafer on Favere's desk and said, "If Captain Kirk is through asking questions, I'd like to talk about Ms. Payton's report."

"I'm through," Kirk said. He steeled himself for what was to come.

"Would you like to start, Commodore?"

"No, thank you, Mr. Kent. You go right ahead."

Kirk shifted in his chair. This overly polite passing him up and back made him nervous and a little irritable. He felt like "it" in a game of keep-away.

Kent harrumphed and cleared his throat. He picked up the blue wafer again and held it delicately between thumb and forefinger. When he had everyone's attention he said, "I must admit that the contents of this report came as a surprise to me."

Kent was silent for a long time, but his comment did not seem to merit a reply.

Kent went on. "And though I am not pleased, I *am* moved by this amazing story. Miracles indeed!" He smiled philosophically and shook his head.

What was Kent getting to? Kirk wondered.

Kent contemplated Kirk for a moment and then said, "I know what you think of me, Kirk. You think I am a bombastic old fool who has taken on Starfleet only to attract attention, to get myself named president of the Federation Council."

Kirk could not help smiling at the accuracy of Kent's analysis.

"But," Kent went on, "you're wrong. It's true that I am a politician, and I look for the main chance. As a starship captain you can certainly appreciate that."

"Certainly." They were just two men of the galaxy agreeing on obvious principles of life that eluded lesser folk.

"But though I am stubborn, I am not stupid. When somebody shows me facts I weigh them, and, if necessary, I change my mind." He set the blue wafer on the desk and tapped it with one finger. "This changes my mind."

"Meaning what?" McCoy asked impatiently.

"Meaning first, that I regret my association with Professor Omen. I knew nothing of his attacks. Still, if in any way I encouraged him to destroy the ships of any species, I made a tragic error."

"You didn't know," Payton said. "Even Omen admitted that."

"Oh, yes," Kent said, "One may make excuses. If I had supported Omen in his activities, I guarantee that I would have been smarter than to send Hazel Payton out to investigate." He chuckled and shook his head.

"And second?" Favere asked.

"Second," Kent said, "I am very impressed by Captain Kirk's actions in this matter. Swift thinking and best use of available equipment allowed *Enterprise* to escape from the pocket universe. You did not destroy the Klingee ship even when you thought your chances of doing so were good. You offered Professor Omen a chance to surrender and, according to Ms. Payton's report, were genuinely upset when he chose not to accept your offer. I admit it, Captain. I am impressed."

Kirk was so surprised by Kent's speech, he was not sure he'd heard right. He said, "Mr. Kent, you overwhelm me."

"I'm sure I do, Captain." He turned to Ms. Payton and said, "You know what this means, don't you?"

Payton's grin had broadened during Mr. Kent's speech. After all, she knew what was in her report. Only her boss's reaction to it had been in doubt. She said, "Don't make me guess, sir."

"Very well. My dear, it appears that I've been wrong about Starfleet. It is now obvious to me that its members are not all boneheads and warmongers. Many of them are intelligent peacekeepers with the best interests of the Federation at heart. Prominent among these sterling souls is Commodore Favere. If you want to marry him, you have my blessing."

Favere dropped the bullet. It rolled to the edge of the desk and onto the floor, but he did not move to pick it up. He was transfixed.

Payton took Kent's hand in hers and said, "Thank you, Conrad. I don't need your approval, but it's nice to know I have it."

Kent took back his hand and waved a finger at her. Gruffly, as if embarassed by his own benevolence, he said, "But you can plan your wedding later. At the moment, we have a more immediate problem."

"Of course," said Ms. Payton. "You can't accuse Starfleet of warmongering any longer. You'll need a new cause."

"I'm afraid our problem is more extensive than that. Damage control is necessary."

"Your little joke on the Klingons," Kirk said.

Kent looked at Kirk with amazement.

Kirk said, "The Klingons lodged a formal protest with the Federation. Keeping that sort of thing quiet is difficult. Admiral Nogura and I discussed it."

"Yes. I'm afraid my thoughtless words cost me the presidency." He sighed.

"I'm sorry, Conrad," Payton said, and she touched his hand.

"I brooded about it while you were gone, and I'm starting to get used to the idea." Still frowning, he stared at the floor. He looked at Payton and said, "But I'm still a councilor, and that still counts for something." He shrugged. "Maybe I can still do some good."

"Of course you can still do good," McCoy said. "Days ago I suggested an area that needs work."

Kent stared at McCoy and said, "You interest me, strangely. What was this area?"

It delighted Kirk that Kent had either forgotten what McCoy had said or had not listened to him in the first place.

McCoy said, "I told you: The methods the Starfleet Medical Corps uses to approve new drugs and medical techniques are over twenty-five years old!"

"Important stuff," Payton said. "Noble stuff."

"Indeed it is, Ms. Payton." Kent stood and said, "Come, Dr. McCoy. Walk with me."

"Captain?"

"Go ahead, Bones." As Kirk watched Kent and McCoy leave together he realized that Starfleet now had a powerful friend where once it had a powerful enemy. Errors in judgment could sometimes be corrected by someone willing to admit he was wrong, even while those errors prevented someone from becoming president. Kirk could not make up his mind about Kent.

In any case, McCoy had been right about Payton all along. Sometimes being a romantic worked out.

Kirk stood and said, "Mr. Spock, I believe the meeting is over."

"Unless the commodore has anything further to discuss."

Favere was lost in Ms. Payton's eyes.

"Commodore?" Spock said.

Favere jumped as if he'd been awakened. "No, Mr. Spock. We have nothing further to discuss."

Still, Spock seemed reticent to leave. Kirk was sure it seemed to him that many questions had been dropped without being fully examined. But unless someone insisted they return to business, Payton and Favere were obviously content to consider other things. There would be time for Mr. Spock's questions, time, as some poet once said, "to murder and create." Eventually any board of inquiry would certainly be required to talk about those things; after all, murder and creation had been Omen's line of work.

Kirk said, "Come on, Spock. Let's go mind the store."

THE LONG-AWAITED FIRST ORIGINAL NOVEL BASED ON THE CRITICALLY ACCLAIMED TELEVISION SHOW

#1 ALIEN NATION™

THE DAY OF DESCENT

THE NEW NOVEL BY JUDITH AND GARFIELD REEVES-STEVENS

ALIEN NATION: a ground-breaking and thought-provoking television program that introduced the TENCTONESE, or NEW-COMERS, a race of aliens and former slaves who have landed on Earth and now comprise the world's newest and strangest group of immigrants.

THE DAY OF DESCENT is the incredible—never before seen—story of the Newcomers' first landing. The year is 1995 and a Tenctonese slave ship is headed for Earth and a landing in the California desert. As Earth awaits its first encounter with an alien race, the Tenctonese are battling for their freedom. Suddenly, two men—destined to be partners—must work together for the first time—with the survival of both their peoples hanging in the balance.

POCKET
STAR
BOOKS

Available from Pocket Star Books

632-01